CW00967761

DEPORTED

First published in
2023
All Rights Reserved
R.G. Winchester
https://makeusmileprints.com
Illustrations by
R.G.Winchester

I dedicate this book to all the people that I have met at The Club International de Nerja who have now become lifelong friends.

Look for the next instalment:

The Man With Three Names

Chapter One

Light penetrated through the bedroom blinds, showering the room into thousands of piercing shards of sunlight. It was unseasonably warm for June, with no forecast of rain. Lilian, although awake, sleep still prevailed. It took very little effort to gaze at the rainbow of colours from her upstairs bedroom window that originated from plants collected around the world. There were important things to do this morning, including chatting to Daisy and checking if Professor Celeriac's migraine was still affecting his taste and smell. Once downstairs, bouncing like a rubber ball, she flew from the conservatory, keeping to the paved path and into the jungle of plants. Some of them had open mouths while their eyes were closed and all were catching the first rays of the morning sun.

Professor Celeriac's eyes were open, but Lilian thought he wasn't awake. As she thought Carperhanus was asleep she turned.

'You okay, Professor?'

He yawned. 'Hmmm my migraine has gone. Now my back feels it has been kicked by a large pink donkey!'

'A large pink donkey! Where are you coming from? Maybe you ought to take some of that stuff that I gave you because it works wonders,' said Lilian.

Carperhanus's eyelids flickered as Lilian made her way further into the garden. Most of the plants were aware of her presence and even the new arrivals wanted to say hello in their own friendly way.

After greeting them all, it wasn't long before Lilian returned to Carperhanus and she spoke slowly.

'When I came by earlier you seemed to be asleep.'

'No, I heard your footsteps, I was just thinking about the past and how quickly time goes.'

'That sounds interesting, tell me more, I have nothing else planned for today.'

'It's a story that will take far too long. You will only get bored and the new arrivals will want to get to know you, as you wander around your garden.'

'I will give them my full attention later, I promise. Please Carperhanus, tell me the story. I won't get bored. I will be as quiet as a mouse and listen to your story.

'All right then. Take a seat. So… Many, many years ago this place that we call home was invaded by foreign soldiers. The rumour was that they came from a place called Rome, wherever that is. The invading army was lead by, Marcus Carperhanus. He was a brute of a soldier with olive skin and almond eyes. He was strong, cunning and very wise. That is why he was chosen to invade and lead four, or was it five legions of fighting men, in unknown territory. Through time, that is how the name was passed down to me. Sometime much later, I am not exactly sure when, but the earth's climate began to change dramatically. Nowadays the change is our invisible invader. Inside the Arctic Circle the exodus of the population was due to a permanent freeze. Marcus Carperhanus will tell you of the scrapes and antics of the Dead End Gang along with the Scrap Yard Kids as they fled from their frozen island to a different way of life where the weather was kinder to the population. With the population from parts of the world on the move they were all looking for somewhere drier, warmer or cooler and wetter. Are you still listening to me? If not, I won't continue.'

'Yes, of course I am. Yes go on.

Carperhanus

Carperhanus is an extremely large plant with what appears to have a pointed chin. He can be grumpy at times. He is known to all in the garden as know all. Been around a thousand years, so they say. Lilian always has a good conversation with him and they never argue. His ears can pick up the slightest of sounds.

4

Chapter Two

The world's weather changed. Sea levels rose. The hot areas of the world were getting drier and hotter, and the cold frozen areas have become impossible to live in. Hot continents need water, cold areas need heat. Something had to change.

The Dead End Gang

The Pope: He was a born leader and he took after his mother for he was big, round and clever. From an early age he was nosy, argumentative, bossy and to some, a bully. However, deep down he had a heart of gold. If he slept outdoors looking at the night sky, his passion was counting the stars. Once asleep there was no waking him up.

Joey Pear: She was the Pope's cousin from his father's side. Her brain was wired like a computer and everyone knew her as, Pear Brain, which she loved. She was forceful and a deep thinker. She hated the rain and the cold. Two things she did every day was to drink a cup of tea first thing in the morning and one just before bed.

Bok Choy: Nobody had any idea how Bok ended up with a name like that. Some say he was a one armed man who sold fruit and vegetables. Everybody thought his brain contained nothing but sawdust. Often he would laugh at his own jokes. He had a knack of being able to sleep anywhere, even upside down if he had to. Almost every day something would go missing, never to be seen again.

Charlie Parsnip: He would have loved to be called just Charlie or Charles. The image he portrayed was a rough and tough enforcer character. He had a brain that was sharp as a razor blade. A long distance runner, he could run twenty, thirty, forty, miles without shoes. He never mentions his family or where he originally came from and when he retired to bed he always wears his hat.

Even though time froze years ago, nobody knew why they were called the Dead End Gang. However, they lived on a flat frozen Island known as Icicle Island, just inside the Arctic Circle. It was so cold you could walk on water and the wind was on occasions, so strong it could blow people over. The sun came out once, but never again. With very little to eat and no warm clothes to wear, The Pope, Joey Pear, Bok Choy and Charlie Parsnip hatched a plan and decided to leave the island on a wooden sledge with a huge sail that they hoped would moved them along the ice at the speed of a bullet. They took with them, hot soup and stale bread and dripping and with enough money to last three days if they were lucky. It would have helped if they had had a compass showing in which direction to go. Therefore, with more luck than judgement, they suddenly appeared so quietly, nobody knew they were there at the bottom of Lilian's secret garden! Not even Lilian!

Soon, the four travellers' grubby, sticky fingers were into everything. Some good. Some not so good. It was not long before everybody, young and old knew them. Most of those already in the garden wanted to know their age, but it was a secret document protected by the MI5 and few knew of its existence. It did not take the four of them long to adapt to the warmer climate but they had terrible trouble getting out of bed in the morning. Winter or summer it made no difference.

Because on Icicle Island everything froze solid, it was safer to stay in bed. Perhaps it was because they never went to sleep until gone midnight because there was too much talking and laughing, mostly about nothing! It would often be well after 10 o'clock in the morning before they were all up and ready

The Pope

The Pope was a born leader. He took after his mother. Big round and clever. From an early age he was nosy, argumentative, quite bossy and to some a bully, but deep down he had a heart of gold. If he slept outdoors looking at the night sky, his passion was to count the stars. Once asleep there was no waking him up.

for a day of ducking and diving, to increase their wealth. All four of them had no set working hours, they just pleased themselves. Somedays it was good and other days it was not.

Lots of things changed after they left Frozen Island. When they did go to bed, The Pope slept out in the open unless it was raining, laying on his back looking at the millions of twinkling stars that he would have liked to have touched. Often he would try to count them, but could not get past 176 before the shutters came down on his eyes. He was a heavy sleeper and didn't he snore!

Joey Pear could not stand the rain or the cold so she always went to bed in Mr. Toadstool's old house. It was lovely and dry and if she lit the fire she was asleep as soon as she closed her eyes. The house had been empty for years. She tended the garden and did all the painting and she could not be happier. She paid rent for the house but it was silly money, and as she had never seen or met Mr Toadstool, she had never paid anybody a single penny. Being an accountant her rent was put away each week. It was so well hidden, sometimes even she forgot where she had put it.

Bok Choy could sleep anywhere, even upside down if he had to. He was most comfortable sliding into an old wine bottle making sure there was no wine or creepy crawlies inside. Once comfortable, he would then pulled the cork with a piece of string to close the door. That seemed to stop the wind and the rain. Then to open it he simply pushed it with his foot, although he had to be careful not to turn over in bed too quickly, because being in a bottle it was prone to roll. Once he found himself too close to the river! Another two or three inches and he could have been a glass submarine! And Bok Choy had never learnt to swim. Now that did frighten him!! Once, half asleep, he got up in the middle of the night, he put the cork in the door to keep out anything unwanted. Being dark he could not find the bottle, then he couldn't get in, as the door only opened from the inside. Silly Bok Choy.

To be different, Charlie Parsnip liked to sleep upright, with his head just above the top of the soil. He would find a spot just under a tree or bush, scoop out the sandy soil and make a nice round hole, just big enough to slide into. With his woolly hat to keep his head warm and boots keeping his feet worm, he was nice and dry. What he did not like was to be disturbed once his eyes were closed as he would always be out for the count.

As soon as his eyes opened, The Pope had to eat breakfast before anything else. Anything would do but not eggs, as they would bring him out in yellow spots!

Joey Pear would check the bank account first, every morning while the kettle was boiling. Then she would look to see if any money had arrived overnight, and then strong tea and toast was all she wanted.

Once Bok Choy was up, the first thing he did was to make sure nothing had gone missing or had got lost, and that took some time! Once, he accused everybody of touching his tin of Brylcreem, only to discover he had been putting it on his feet as a cure for chilblains. Then two chocolate bars were always eaten very quickly, and they were followed by a large number of fizzy drinks.

As soon as Charlie Parsnip was awake he would go for a run, twenty miles or more, without wearing boots. Always when he got back, The Pope would say, 'Wash your feet, they don't half stink!' Usually, Charlie took no notice. He never ate breakfast.

There was not a day passed when Bok Choy would lose or mislay something, maybe a shoe or a shirt. Once it was a false tooth. Often it was his watch, although it didn't work as no one had any idea how to put a new battery in it. The other three often thought that Bok Choy could do with a new battery. The kind that prolonged your life and give you a jump start in the morning.

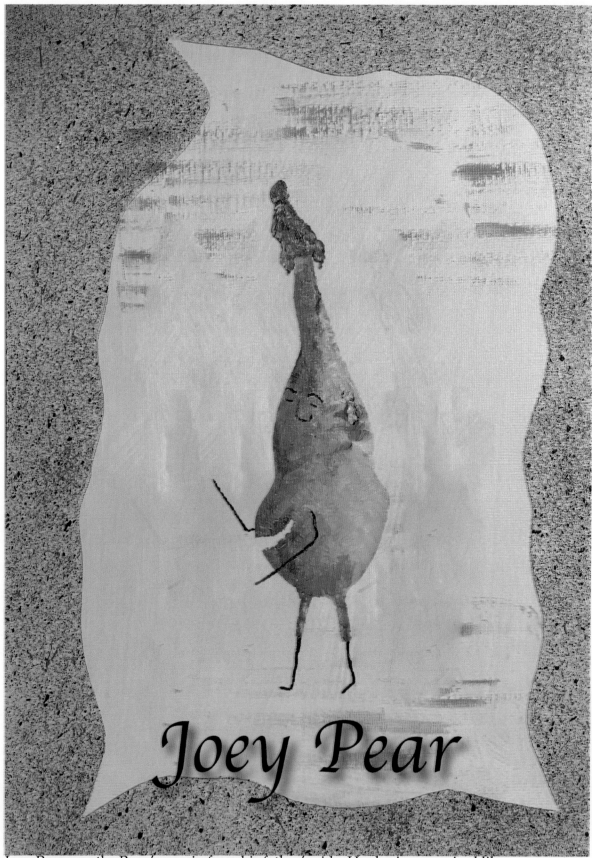

Joey Pear

Joey Pear was the Pope's cousin from his father's side. Her brain was wired like a computer and everyone knew her as Pear Brain, which she loved. She was quite forceful and a deep thinker. She hated the rain and the cold. Two things she did every day was she drank a cup of tea first thing in the morning and one just before bed.

While they were waiting for Bok Choy, Charlie Parsnip looked at the other two.

'Did you hear that explosion early this morning? It was deafening! I had only gone about half a mile. Then two cop cars came flying up the road. I suspect it will be in the local paper this week giving detailed descriptions of whatever it was.'

Bok Choy was listening to this then said, 'I am not going to get the local paper, the man in the shop shouted at me, "you stupid imbecile". So I shouted back, "If you call me an imbecile again I will give you a good clip around the ear." That made him go all red in the face.'

A New Day

It was a crisp dry morning and was going to be hot today as the sun moved over the tall trees at the side of a quiet country lane.

'Now we have to go and pick up two boxes of old used toothbrushes from a friend of a friend,' said The Pope.

'Who is going to clean them?' shouted Joey Pear.

The Pope was smiling as he said, 'Bok Choy of course.'

With a rather sad face, Bok Choy coughed and said, 'Why have I got to clean the old used toothbrushes? Can't someone else do the dirty work for a change?'

Charlie Parsnip asked, 'What are we going to do with them once Bok Choy has cleaned and made them look like new?'

'Re-sell them. There's a good profit to be made,' said, The Pope still smiling. Bok Choy wanted to know if the bristles on the tooth brushes were all going to go one way and how do we straighten them up. The Pope replied, 'We don't. There is a new design meant to get into all the tight spaces. Assuming they had teeth with lots of gaps.'

'How far is it to walk, because my legs are aching and I'm having trouble making them work even though I have given them a good oil and grease up?' asked Joey Pear.

'About two miles and the walk will do us all good,' said the Pope.

Charlie Parsnip shouted, 'we should have brought the trolley and then the boxes wouldn't have to be carried. You do know it's all uphill?'

Immediately Joey Pear said, 'Well if my legs won't work, I could jump up on the trolley.'

'Pulling you and the boxes up hill, you are having a laugh.'

Bok Choy said, 'Where is the hill? I see no hill, but I can spot a cake shop. The sign reads, Taylor's freshly baked bread, rolls and quality cakes. Open every day but not Friday, Saturday or Sunday. "Special offer, stale cakes half price" Let's treat ourselves and go in and buy big fat doughnuts on this hot and sticky morning.'

The Pope became flustered and ordered, 'no doughnuts, they make you fat and lazy. Do be quiet you lot and let's get a move on, I don't want to be late and also the exercise will do us all good.'

With a lot of huffing and puffing, all four eventually got close to the top of the hill.

Joey Pear looked at, The Pope and said, 'What is that?' If she had have been on her own, she would have been frightened.'

Standing still with two dirty boxes was the thinnest thing anybody had ever seen.

'Good morning. I'm called, The Stick. Which one of you is, The Pope?'

'I'm, The Pope. Have you got the goods, because I hope we have not come all this way for nothing. First I want to look at the brushes. I am expecting toothbrushes not paintbrushes.'

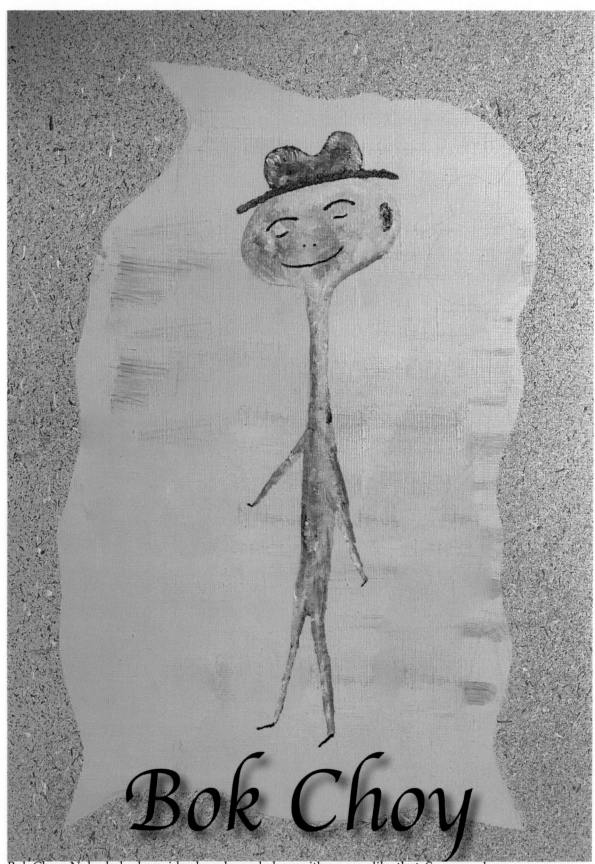

Bok Choy

Bok Choy: Nobody had any idea how he ended up with a name like that. Some say he was a one armed man who sold fruit and veg. Everybody thought his brain contained loads of sawdust. Often he would laugh at his own jokes. He had a knack of being able to sleep anywhere, even upside down if he had to. Almost every day something would go missing, never to be seen again.

'Well I didn't think you would clean your teeth with paint brushes, you silly old fool. You can look but don't touch, they are all yours when I get my money,' said, The Stick.

Out of the corner of The Pope's eye, was another strange looking creature. He wondered who it was. Staring at, The Stick, The Pope said, ' Is that thing with you?'

'Don't mind him. Yes he is with me. A sort of bodyguard, cum chauffeur, come, personal assistant. He is one of those strong silent types. I call him, Heave Ho. He is harmless really, but don't touch him. He hates to be touched, so don't get too close.'

Whispering, Charlie Parsnip said, 'I would not want to meet, Heave Ho on a dark night, thank you very much.'

The old toothbrushes were inspected by, The Pope, and Joey Pear was told to give the cash to, The Stick.

'It's all there, would you like to count it?'

With his tongue sticking out he said, 'it won't be necessary, you have got to have some trust', as he passed the cash to Heave Ho, the personal assistant.

The Stick then said, 'before you go, one more thing, would you be interested in twenty sets of false teeth? They have hardly been used, perhaps some soup, the odd meat pie and loads of jelly and custard. There is no chewing. It slides down and they will never be missed.'

Before The Pope and The Stick could speak, Bok Choy said, 'We don't want them and I refuse to clean old false teeth with bits of food stuck between them or make sure they work.'

His face turned red as The Pope shouted, 'take no notice of him. Are the teeth in good condition? I can't sell them if some are missing or broken. Have any of them come from a smoker? How much do you want?'

The Stick's face broke into a smile. 'The last owners could hardly talk or eat, let alone smoke. To you, a giveaway price.'

He gave, The Pope a bag of old yellow false teeth that Heave Ho had hidden in his pocket. They looked okay, almost like new as The Pope peered onto the bag. Now, The Pope was smiling. He began looking first at the assistant, Heave Ho and then The Stick saying, 'are you sure they won't be missed?'

'No, we sell new ones, buy one get one free, I can assure you that the previous owners will not miss them. They will have no need for false teeth where they are going.'

Once again Joey Pear looked at, The Stick as the money was handed over, which went into Heave Ho's deep pockets. Before you could blink, The Stick and his assistant turned and ran like greased lightning, leaving The Dead End Gang with secondhand toothbrushes and a bag of old false teeth. The Pope watched them disappear and then thought, I hope I have not been duped.

Back Home

Charlie Parsnip, who had not said much, looked directly at The Pope and asked, 'what is the plan to get rid of these items?'

With a red face ,The Pope said, 'it's quite simple, we sell them to our local dentist, Doctor Paul Harder. Some of his patients will take anything, especially if the price is right. Paul has certainly got the gift of the gab, especially after we have cleaned and polished them, they will look brand new and that will make a nice profit for us.'

Charlie Parsnip

Charlie Parsnip: He would have loved to be called just Charlie or Charles. The image he portrayed was a rough and tough enforcer character. He had a brain that was sharp as a razor blade. A long distance runner, he could run twenty, thirty, forty, miles with no shoes on. He never mentions family or where he originally came from. When he goes to bed it is always with his hat on.

Making their way back home with the goods, three of them started to grumble. Joey Pear complained her legs didn't work while Bok Choy kept on about cleaning the brushes and the teeth.

Charlie Parsnip said more than once, 'should have brought a trolley, should have brought a trolley.'

Joey Pear shouted, 'I could have got on the trolley to save my legs.'

The Pope finally shouted, 'be quiet you lot. Give it a rest.'

Once at home, The Pope began to issue his orders.

'Fill a large bucket with hot soapy water, no bleach because it makes the teeth go black and then we would have to give them a coat of white paint. Start cleaning the brushes and the teeth. One of you dry them and the other make sure the teeth all fit together, I can't sell false teeth if they don't match. I am going to find the dentist.'

When he found him. the Dentist, Dr Paul Harder shouted at, The Pope.

'I have waited here ten minutes and was just about to go. You forget I have a room full of patients.' Nonetheless, looking at the brushes and teeth and speaking with a wide grin on his face said, 'excellent goods,' passing over the cash to, The Pope.

'You will find false teeth in the box with the brushes. They have hardly been used. Ice cream, jelly and custard. That sort of thing. Definitely no curry, garlic or smokers. To you, a giveaway price. If you like them you can add the cash to our next bit of business, and don't worry…they will never be missed.'

In a flash, the dentist was gone with his goods. When The Pope returned, Charlie Parsnip asked, 'what's next?' Bok Choy said his mate's father had a bag of glass eyes, that had never been used. They looked alright, bright and nice and shiny. Looking at, The Pope who still had a red face, he asked, 'what are we to do with them, you stupid thing?'

Bok Choy explained that they come in all colours; green, blue, and brown. Large, medium or small. He told them they are easy to fit. 'All you have to do is pull your eyelid up and pop it in. A bit like dropping a tea bag into a cup of hot water. Of course, making sure, they are not back to front and with the right colour. Because you would look very silly if you got it wrong. We could try and sell them as marbles. If you played with them you would have an advantage because they could see where they were going.'

The Pope walked away shaking his head as he mumbled to himself, 'I think Bok Choy has lost his marbles.'

The other two were bent over laughing as, The Pope turned he shouted over his shoulder, 'I am going to find the invisible man.' Bok Choy turned to the other two, 'I am only trying to help. What The Pope lacks is vision. Why doesn't anybody take me seriously?'

Later at night

Still shaking his head, The Pope thought glass eyes that can see where they are *going?* Whatever next? The Pope walked as quickly as he could past some rundown houses, that were unoccupied. They had all been vandalised, right up to the railway line at the bottom of the road, where he had seen or thought he had seen the invisible man before.

Actually, there were two invisible men but, The Pope did not know this, one acquired the goods the other sold them, and the two were very secretive and so very hard to find. There had been a rumour going around that nobody had ever seen their faces and had no idea where they lived or where they came from. Most wondered how to get in touch with them. If you were in the know it was easy. If you

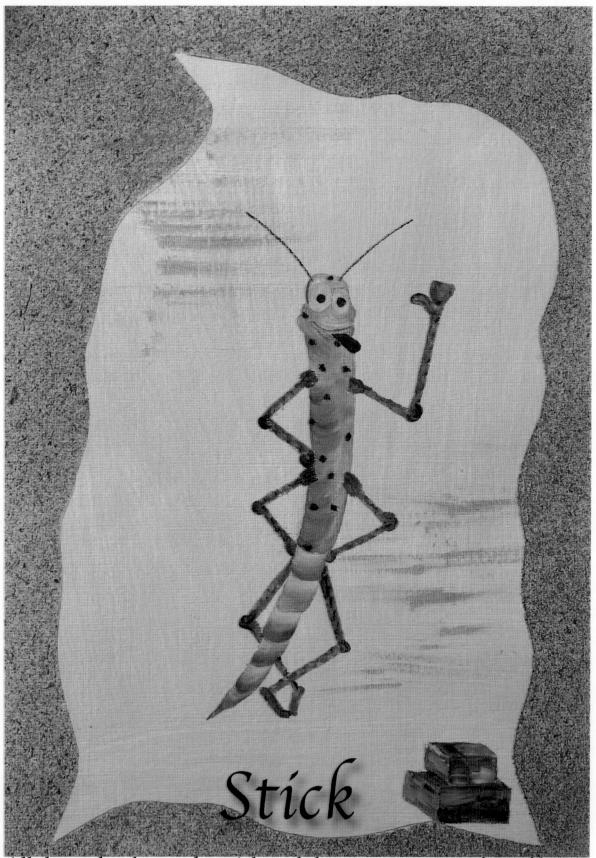

Stick

All those that knew the stick and there were quite a few, if he eat any food. He had his fingers into many pies. This made him very popular.

were looking to buy, you just rang a mobile number which would then give you another number. If you were looking to sell you would call a different number. These numbers changed every week. That's how they got to be known as the invisible pair.

Finally, The Pope reached the railway line. Looking around it seemed deserted. It was dark but not late. Nobody was walking around with their dog. It was as quiet as a graveyard. He wondered if he was being watched. He dialled both numbers, and a rough voice answered, 'yes?'

'Pope here…any bargains going spare?'

After a silence that lasted for a minute or two the rough voice said, 'so it's you again, Pope, how did you get on with that sulphuric acid? If you have any left over I will give you a good price. Think about it. Now I have got two trays of winkles going cheap. They came in fresh two days ago I think and have got to be eaten by tomorrow.'

The Pope instantly agreed on a price over the phone, saying he would send one of his gang to pick them up at ten o'clock that night. He knew the invisible men had a helper known as Shifty. Shifty by name shifty by nature, who could not speak a word of English, using sign language only.

As The Pope hurried back he would get Bok Choy to meet this Shifty character at ten, exchange the cash for the winkles and get back as soon as possible. Joey Pear would then fill a tub with ice that, The Pope got from a friend, then he would ask Charlie Parsnip to go and wake up the fish bloke, Joe Stinker, who lived above the shop, five minutes from the station and would tell him, 'If he is in bed shout out, "The Pope has got fresh winkles for you, half price." Don't tell him where they come from or how old they are.'

'I don't like touching them winkles,' shouted Charlie Parsnip. 'I read somewhere if you look at them they can wink back at you. I don't like the idea of all them winkles winking at me. Are they dead or alive? Because if they are alive they might want to come out and have a look around.'
'They have not got any eyes, stupid,' shouted, The Pope.

'Well, how do they know where they are or if it was day or night?'

'Just go and get rid of the winkles. If you are frightened just close your eyes. What would be a good idea would be if I could have two of the glass eyes that Bok Choy's friend has got then I would not be able to see the winkles.'

'Give him the winkles, count the cash. It should all be there. Don't lose any of it. You may also ask him if he would like fresh crabs.'

'You will have to get one of the others. I can't touch them crabs, they have got long pinchers. I don't like being pinched by them pinchers and they have two big black eyes that pop out at you.'

'Look, these crabs are unique. They don't have any pinchers, also their eyes are like moulded glass. Very special these crabs. Half price if he takes a box. Almost forgot, tell him I have two dozen whelks. They are a bit tough and so to get rid of them, best sell them to old people with no teeth. They can suck them as they are too tough to chew.'

It was quite late, when back at base Joey Pear had already gone to bed. The Pope would get Joey Pear to bank the cash tomorrow then speaking to the other two quietly, 'let's all of us have a day off tomorrow. I will put a note through Joey Pear's letter box to let her know our plans and let's meet up at ten o'clock tomorrow morning.'

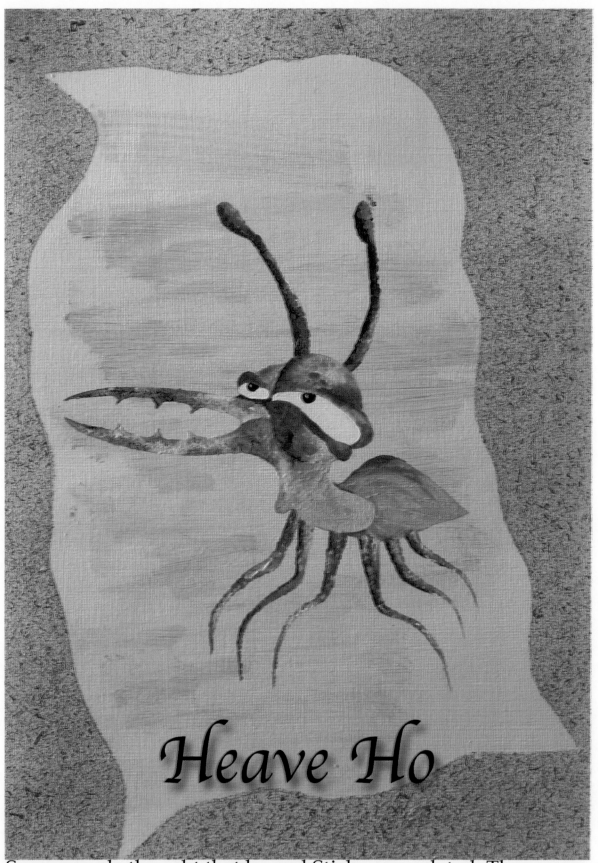

Heave Ho

Some people thought that he and Stick were related. They were very close but Stick was the boss and H H, as he was known, was the enforcer.

Chapter Three

The Scrap Yard Kids

The Arctic air became so cold it was impossible to breath. More and more of the population moved away from the island. Trees had stopped growing so there was very little wood, and vegetables froze in the ground. The ice became so thick you could not break it to go fishing. In the middle of the island, four friends who went to school together became known as the Scrap Yard Kids. In their spare time, they would collect rubbish that lay around the island ready for recycling. Plastic, scrap metal paper and cardboard large or small, they collected it all, but it became so cold the metal froze, making it impossible to move. Jointly their plan was to leave the frozen island, along with others. They hoped to have found enough wood and metal to build an open container, strong enough to hold four of them, attaching it to a huge balloon, made out of bits of plastic, rubber and nylon sheeting. When they were ready, they stuffed their bags with fizzy drinks, milk, goats cheese sandwiches with piccalilli, a rusty compass, a torch for when it got dark, but forgot the batteries. At last they had formulated a draft plan. Do it now or they would never leave this frozen Island. With the wind howling, four tethered ropes would be cut, when the wind was in the right direction. They could float up into the clouds, all shouting together, 'Bye-bye frozen island.'

They had heard of a secret garden from a friend of a friend who knew the Dead End Gang, but had no idea where it was. They found their old compass was not working, maybe because of rust, dirt, and lack of oil. Climbing into the open rickety container, they cut the ropes and then the balloon was moving them along as fast as a jet plane. It was then discovered the balloon had developed a small hole in the nylon sheeting, which was impossible to repair up in the sky. As they came slowly down the one thing they all knew was that they were thousands of miles off course, and In the dark with no batteries in their torch. Fortunately it was just starting to get light.

The small hole in the side of the balloon suddenly appeared to grow in size, making the rickety container fall dangerously fast. The bigger the hole the faster they seemed to fall. Billy Took was going to be sick. He had thoughts of throwing the goat's cheese sandwiches with the piccalilli over the side to lighten the load. As he looked at the other three then shouted 'Hold hands and brace yourself, because very likely we shall crash land on top of that greenhouse!!!' In a squeaky voice, Mercury Boy said, 'I don't want to die yet.'

Copper wanted to say, but could not speak, 'I hope there is nobody in there taking cuttings of plants.'

They held their breath, closed their eyes as the container was now in the lap of the gods. Seconds passed, with trembling hands and wobbly legs, the bang was like a cannon going off. They hit the greenhouse roof full on, smashing the container to bits and completely demolishing the tired old greenhouse in Lilian's sweet scented tropical garden.

Glass, wood, metal, and plastic shattered into a hundred pieces. Plant pots, soil ,flowers and an old established grape vine were reduced to unrecognisable rubble. Copper was the first to open his eyes and after adjusting to the dust and the dirt cried out, 'is everybody ok?'

Mayzack and Mercury Boy were both in shock. Neither could say a word.

Billy Took looked around in disbelief at the destruction. That greenhouse saved our lives, it broke our fall. Seeing the other three badly shaken but with only cuts and bruises said, 'We need to disappear

Paul Harder

The local dentist, doctor Paul harder had lots of patience. He was known to charm the birds out of the trees. Being a local man his surgery was always full. He had known the Pope for many years. Some say they went to school together others said they didn't think so.

18

quickly before the police or worse turned up. Grab your stuff and leave nothing behind, let's leg it before the owners come out of that big house.'

Once outside the garden they jumped, hopped and climbed over an old gate and then scrambled down a narrow lane leading to open fields with a quiet country road and hopefully to safety. It must have been a strange sight to see four kids hobbling and running as fast as their legs would go, looking as though they had been in an explosion. Suddenly, Billy Took dived into the tall bushes at the side of the road quickly followed by the other three. Minutes passed as they held their breath listening for the 'da-da, da-da'. Just then, two police cars raced past at breakneck speed. No words were spoken but all four knew where they were heading. Once the noise of the siren had died away, the four laid quite still trying their best to relax and breathe normally.

Billy Took said, 'I think we should stay put. It's not ideal but at least we are hidden, and whoever called the police must be wondering why a homemade balloon and a smashed up, rickety container, with no one in it, would smash into the greenhouse.'

Mercury Boy looked up. 'I am hungry!! Our goat's cheese sandwiches have been squashed to smithereens. Now what are we going to eat?'

'Be quiet,' whispered, Copper as they lay there. It became obvious that there were voices that were getting louder.

Listening they heard, 'my feet ache. I told you to bring a trolley. If you want them cleaned, do it yourself!'

'Be quiet you lot.'

After a while Mayzack whispered, 'what was all that about and did any of you recognise them? Because I'm sure they are trouble. Could they be the gang that roamed our island?'

Billy Took said, 'I don't know, I have never seen them before, but we could follow them and see where they go, we may be able to get some new clothes and some food.'

Mercury Boy said, 'good idea, I am starving.'

Mayzack agreed. Copper thought Mayzack was the same. 'You are always starving.'

Following at a safe distance it became clear all four of the Dead End Gang lived very close together. It was Toadstool House that came into view first, and close by was an old wine bottle. All four had the same thought; how could anybody sleep in there? Staying out of sight they could still hear what was being said.

Laying still as lumps of wood, Billy Took said, 'let's stick with them and see what takes place. Let's go but keep down and remember to be quiet. What we don't want is them knowing that we are following and spying on them.'

Billy Took said, 'this gets better and better. Mayzack? Follow him, the one they call, Bok Choy. See who he meets and what he does, but don't let them see you. You do understand?' Mayzack nodded. He turned and disappeared into the darkness. 'Okay, now let's keep our heads down and no talking.'

19

Shifty

Shifty was one of life's troubled characters. Deaf, dumb but crafty. He knew how many beans make five. Shifty took no liberties from anyone.

Chapter Four

A Day off

The day began late, very late. The first one up was Charlie Parsnip, out for his morning jog, no shoes on as usual. The other two were up but both knew that Joey Pear was still in bed with a cup of tea. She would have a late brunch after she had checked the bank account. She was a stickler for routine. After a few jobs and more tea, it was time to wander down to see Blossom. She was one of Joey's closest friends, about forty years of age but she looked much younger. If she had not got such big hooter, you may have called her glamourous. Joey did not know if that was her first or second name. There was more tea and gossip until both had sore throats. Then it was back to Toadstool House for dinner and lighting the fire if it was cold.

'Ah, Bok Choy? What are your plans today?' asked, The Pope, as he was looking for his shoelaces. He had both shoes on but on the wrong feet.

'Well, when I find my laces I am going to search for my lost, Uncle Joe; the one that is 102. I told you about him, cranky old fool. As I have said before, he is as mad as a March hare. Reading and writing was never his strong point, sometimes he is deaf but mostly he doesn't know what day it is. Actually he is harmless, but people take him for a doddering old fool, which is a shame.'

'Yes, I remember. Nutty as a fruit cake, that's what you used to say. Is he lost?'

'Not exactly. He was in an old people's home. I received a message to say he has gone missing again. I was there just over two weeks ago if you remember. The home wanted to get rid of him. I can't blame them, smoking that old pipe in bed and setting fire to the bed covers and the curtains. What a mess that made. The fire alarm went off. Most unusual because most of the electrics are either out of date or they have never worked since the house was rewired.

All the old ladies in their nightdresses, outside standing on the lawn, without their teeth in, no slippers on, it must have been a sorry sight. To top it all, two old dears have gone down with pneumonia.

'Do you know why Joe has gone missing this time, and do you have any idea where he has gone?'

'After the fire, they moved him into an old cupboard under the stairs and told him he would be safe from the bombs. That was ok but he would wander around constantly day and night shouting, "Are the bombs coming, you must let me know. Now where did I put my rifle? I had it a minute ago, and I bet Old Tinbag has taken my bullets."'

'No, I said to you before, he used to be a night watchman. He mentioned he wants his job back. He is my relative but I would not trust him with an empty box of matches. I have got to go, I will give you an update later.'

After a ten minute walk, Bok Choy approached the rundown, tired old home and stopped and looked at the upstairs left window which was still covered in black soot from the bedroom fire. He dreaded walking up the broken stone steps to the front door, where the paint was flaking off and the doorbell which if you touched it you could have electrocuted yourself.

There, standing ramrod straight in the doorway and with a face that said, ah it's you again was Miss Tinsnap. 'Come into my office,' she barked.

Walking into the dark damp overcrowded, pokey cold office that smelt of decaying mushrooms and stale cigarette smoke, Bok Choy wished he had now touched the doorbell. He was not offered a seat, not

Joe Stinker

Joe Stinker was an artful bloke. His father and his grandfather were both fishmongers. Joe lived above his shop close to the local railway station. If no females were in his shop his language was very colourful.

that there was much room for a chair. He turned his thoughts to the sloping creaky floor. Should he find himself in the basement, would he ever see daylight again?

Miss Tinsnap was already seated in a chair that looked over three hundred years old and which might collapse imminently. Bok Choy thought about saying it might be safer if I stood. Miss Tinsnap's expression had not changed and if anything she looked more terrifying. As she opened her mouth to speak Bok Choy started to smile and wondered if the dentist, Paul Harder had sold her those stained, yellow secondhand false teeth but his smile faded as she spoke.

'Now look here' she said, 'we cannot put up with your uncle anymore. I lost two members of staff last week. He thought one of them was a chocolate éclair and he wanted to eat her, and thought other one was a parrot. All day long he would shout, "Pretty Polly, Pretty Polly." Then, as you know, he set light to the bed covers smoking that stinking old pipe in bed. I do not want to know what he smokes but it must surely be a health hazard. We have taken the pipe and matches and thrown them in the bin. Now he thinks he is a chicken, standing on the bed waving his arms up and down and jumping into the air to try to fly. You do know he is raving mad? I suggest you go.'

Just then she started to cough. Her face became red and her coughing got louder. Bok Choy wondered again if she had a small marble stuck in her throat, then for a split second thought, was it one of those glass eyes? At least a glass eye could see what was making her cough. No, it's the fifty a day Woodbines that she smokes. Then the coughing stopped as quickly as it started and she said, 'I suggest you go and find him and when you do, don't bring him back here.'

Bok Choy was staring at her thinking you can't just push him out. Then Bok Choy interrupted her.

'We have paid in full up to the end of the month. We demand a refund.'

Then all of a sudden she started to cough again. Bok Choy thought, does she want another Woodbine? If that chair collapses and she ends up on the floor Bok Choy could not give her the kiss of life. Bok Choy burst out laughing. Looking at her terrifying face, he said, 'okay I will find him. He will not be coming back and looking at the state of this home. It is ready to collapse at any moment. You and the rest of the people in this place would end up in the basement.'

Whispering this to myself I muttered, if this place does collapse I hope all the old ladies have their teeth in and their slippers on. When I do find Uncle Joe, I wonder if I could squeeze him into Mr Toadstool's old house with Joey Pear. Thinking again perhaps not.

Mayzack had been gone so long Billy Took thought that he had been perhaps arrested. Copper who was asleep would have to go and find him if he is not back soon. Billy Took had hatched a plan. First, he knew they all needed to sleep. He saw, just up the road was a nice dry barn with running water. That would have to do as a temporary place. All four of them slept like logs, laying on the floor or bales of straw. Thinking back it was sheer luxury compared to where they had lived on Icicle Island.

Mayzack came back puffing and panting it took five minutes to get his breath back, telling the story up to the time of the winkles and crabs. Copper and Mercury Boy looked very nervous. If we get mixed up with that lot the last thing we want is to be returned to Icicle Island. Billy Took said, 'let's sleep on it.'

Bill Swindler

Bill Swindler was a lovely rogue. Liked by all that met him he would buy and sell anything. He had a reputation as a tough cookie. One thing he lacked was he could not read or write but that did not hold him back from making money.

Chapter Five

Mid Morning

As soon as Bok Choy had gone, The Pope turned around to Charlie Parsnip, 'you going out as well, any particular reason?'

'Yep I am just off now going to see an old mate of mine from school. He says he has something that may interest me.'

'Good luck. Don't forget if there is anything of interest let me know. One other thing, does your friend know that the Scrap Yard Kids may have come from our island?'

'I will ask. By the way, what are your plans for the day?' asked Charlie Parsnip.

'Later this morning I am going to call on two blokes that have a reputation for earning a pound or two, Sam Honkey and Dick Dorrey. They have been doing a good line in strange tasting sausages. See you later.'

Buses were few and far between, Charlie Parsnip thought back to Icicles Island as he waited for a number 22 bus to come along. On the Island, nobody could go anywhere, as, it was impossible to see the road. The tires on the buses froze solid so the wheels would not go round. Charlie Parsnip got off at the right stop and waiting for him was his old mate, Bill Swindler. After a quick handshake they went off to get a cup of tea and have a good natter.

Bill was looking around and in a quiet voice, almost a whisper said, 'I can get loads of soap if you are interested, all colours shapes and smells, give away price.'

'Tell me more.' Charlie Parsnip said excitely, raising his voice a little too loudly.

'Not so loud…quietly,' Bill said in a whisper. 'They come in all colours, and sizes but you can't buy one. They come in packs of twenty. It's the smell that makes these so good, not the price. We think they are going to be a big hit. They have been invented by some fella from the continent who can't speak a word of English. I can get almost any smelling soap you fancy. There is soap that will make you smell of fish chips and vinegar, curry smell and there is a new one just out if you fancy smelling like diesel. One that is quite popular is rotten cabbage. They go nuts for that one. Then we have wet smelly socks that is a big hit with the ladies. Can you imagine taking your girlfriend out and she smells of fried onions?'

'Look, let's have another cupper and by the way have you got any samples for me to show and sniff? Our governor, The Pope will want to smell the goods before he parts with any cash.'

'Let me see what I can do but we want our samples back. This is the trendiest thing since sliced bread.'

'No problem,' said Charlie Parsnip, as they drained their tea and continued to chat. Bill then said, 'ask your governor if he wants last year's fireworks. They are all boxed up. They are just a bit out of date. With a felt tipped pen it'll easily be altered.'

Charlie smiled and said,'I will ask.'

Tinsnap

Miss Tinsnap did not like many people. Some say she didn't even like herself. Her devotion to the care home was unique. At times she could be cruel and was never seen without a cigarette.

Chapter Six

The Pope went to see his buddies.

He knew that it was not far to walk, or waddle, due to the access weight, The Pope carried around. He had been trying to lose weight but the cream cakes didn't help. Thinking to himself, I must get rid of some or all of this fat. He arrived at the farm gate slightly out of breath, with his face as red as a beetroot. It should have taken fifteen minutes, not twenty-five. The place looked deserted. 'Hello…' he shouted.

With still no one around, he shouted a second time even louder. He then opened the gate only to be met by two snarling dogs that might have torn him to bits so he stayed this side of the gate. The wind had got up with fine rain falling, so he thought,, this is a waste of time, I could do with a nice cup of tea.

Suddenly, a voice shouted, 'Hello, Pope do come in. The dogs are locked away, you are quite safe. Have you come about the sausages?'

The Pope thought, well I haven't come all this way to wear out my old clothes.

'Yes I have.'

Opening the gate, he instantly trod muck and whatever else was laying on the floor became stuck to his new shoes.

'It's only muck, it will soon wash off,' came the laughing reply.

Looking at his shoes and the bottom of his trousers, The Pope was not laughing.

Mr Honkey, with The Pope, walked up a very muddy path, turned left, and entered a closed porch. It was then suggested that they cover their shoes with plastic bags. Before looking at the sausages, once inside this monstrous building, The Pope thought, 'wow!' you could get lost in here. He was led to a room at the far end of the factory that smelled of disinfectant. As he entered the room, laid out in front of him in neat rows were hundreds of cooked sausages of all shapes, sizes, and colours with as many smells. Looking past the sausages over in the corner sitting on an old wooden box, stuffing his face was Mr Dorrey, a plump man in his late forties. With his mouth full he pointed to, The Pope

'Hi, help yourself, I will be with you in a minute, just finishing my breakfast, We have all flavours. This one that I am eating is particularly nice. Roast duck and coffee flavour. Try that one over there. It is beetroot and grey squirrel, that's a good seller. Another favourite is, minced donkey with Chinese glow worms, a very unusual flavour. It's a bit dearer than some. That's because the cost of the glow worms has rocketed but well worth it.'

The Pope was given a printout of their best sellers with a price list as he chewed on a red worm and butternut squash flavour sausage. The Pope had a smile on his face but inside he wanted to be as sick as a dog. Both Mr Honkey and Mr Dorrey spoke at the same time.

'We started making sausages here about four years ago. We copied the idea from the Chinese who have been doing this for thousands of years. Largely because that was all there was to eat. We have gone from strength to strength. Some of our customers are so well known we could not possibly give you their names. We also export a lot to countries that don't even eat sausages. Before you go, please try this one. It is tripe, beef fat marrowbone jelly. That will stick to your ribs in the winter. There is no salt as it is not good for you. All ingredients are sourced locally where we can and none have any chemicals. We will do you a packet of samples to take home. Let us know what you like. One last thing before you go?

Old Joe
Dicky Rump Don't come back

Old Joe was over 102. Reading and writing was never his strong point. Some say he was slightly eccentric. He could remember the past but not the present. Once you got him to talk there was no stopping him. The care home he went into treated him harshly. Old Joe had three names: Dickie Rump and Don't Come Back were the other two.

The next time you come here there will be an intercom on the gate with a camera. Because we have had people trying to steal our award winning sausages and recipes.'

Thinking on his feet, The Pope asked, 'why not get a night watchman?'

What he didn't say was that the man he had in mind, Joe, was as mad as a March hare. 'Employ him and you won't have anybody trying to steal your sausages. You could get rid of the dogs if you so wish. He didn't say Old Joe can't bite because he has no teeth.

As they looked at ,The Pope, they thought it was a wonderful idea and said would give him a trial run. We will put him on probation for four weeks. His hours and living expenses can be worked out later. We may be able to introduce a bonus scheme, based on how many burglars he can chase off. The Pope did not like the idea but agreed on a wage and then said he would be in touch. All he had to do was to find Joe. How difficult could that be?

Chapter Seven

What made the Scrap Yard kids jump.

As they were listening and watching, they began to drift off to sleep. Out of nowhere stood a tall stocky man in a smart blue suit shouting, 'you three. Stop what are you doing right now!' The Pope looked as white as a ghost. Bok Choy and Charlie Parsnip wanted to turn and run but both knew that their legs would not work. Their mouths were as dry as a cactus.

Again with a booming voice, 'I am Inspector Nickam of the frying pan squad. I know you and your two ruffian mates. Intelligence tells us you were moving into our patch and to expect destruction and robbery. I expect you were responsible for that greenhouse that got blown up. No doubt with some in your homemade gunpowder. I want to know where you got the formula and the ingredients from. Was it homemade or perhaps you got it from a licensed dealer?'

Charlie Parsnip shouted, 'ingredients? We ain't chemists. We have got some salt pepper, red sauce, and a jar of marmalade. We love marmalade sandwiches. Are you saying that if we mix this lot up we will have gunpowder? Don't be so silly.'

'We ain't done nuffink, Mr Nickam and we ain't got no gunpowder, honest.'

'Inspector to you.'

'We heard the bang, we were all in bed at the time, honest, that's all. Why would we want to demolish a greenhouse?'

'Revenge, pay back. I have got my eye on you three. You even smell guilty. Where were you yesterday? Up to no good no doubt. I have got a witness saying that they saw the four of you running down the road going like greased lighting. Come on, own up it will be better for you. Probation will be a lot better than going inside.'

'Look Mr Inspector, we go about our business and we don't cause any trouble, we are a hard working lot us four. Everything we do is within the law. As for gunpowder that is far too dangerous. You do know you can get blown up with that stuff?'

'If you believe that, then you'll believe anything,' shouted the Inspector. 'Only last month I caught two of you with bicycle saddles that weren't yours. You gave me a cock and bull story of a case of mistaken identity. Mistaken identity my foot. I will be back with my witness. Don't go away and don't get lost. Wait a minute, there are four of you lot, so, where is the other one?'

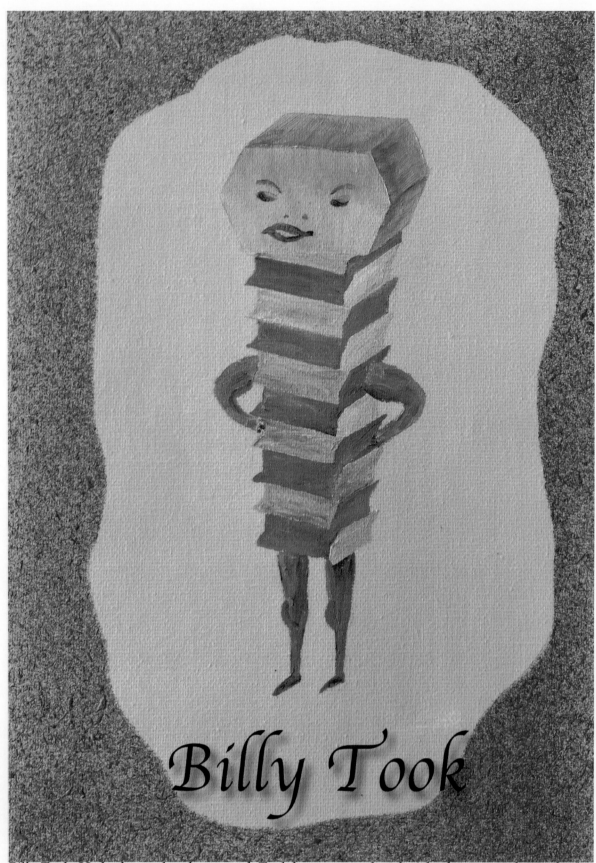

Billy Took

Billy Took: He looks mad and acts mad. Took by name and took risks, by nature, but nobody called him mad. He will often make irrational decisions that go terribly wrong. Once you get to know him he is a very likeable chap. When intelligence was given out they must have missed him, but he has a charm about him that cannot be ignored.

'She has gone to the bank to pay money in, honest money made from hard graft.'

'I don't believe a word you say, so don't make me laugh. You take it out rather than put it in unless there is some scam going on that I don't know about but I intend to find out. That will put a stop to your little racket. I will be back with my witness, which will nail you little lot and then I intend to hang you out to dry.'

Inspector Nickam seemed to disappear as quietly as he arrived. Bok Choy spoke first.

'He won't let go you know. He will be back.'

'Let him come back. He has nothing on us,' murmured, The Pope.

Charlie Parsnip said in a very quiet voice, 'something or someone smashed the greenhouse. As long as we don't get blamed for it that's all that matters.'

The Pope waved his hand, 'as long as it is not pinned on us, I don't care. Let's get back home.'

The story so far: As Lilian went back to the house

Mesmerised by the antics of the eight characters that landed in her garden, time marched on making Lilian's heart race as she was late going back to the house.

Carperhanus opened his eyes wide indicating, don't belong.

As she turned to fly back up the garden path her foot clearly slipped making him shout, 'be careful!!'

It was not long before she bounded out of the conservatory and was back sitting on her upside down flower pot, ready for the rest of the story. A biscuit in one hand, and traces of milk around her mouth.

Carperhanus looking at Lilian said, 'that was quick, I was thinking of having forty winks.'

'Well, you said don't be long.'

Swivelling his head around he saw, four more. Daisy, Delion, Achny the spider and Sidney the snail, sat just behind, very close to Lilian.

'Are you all ready? No interruptions. Now where was I? Inspector Nickam if I remember correctly.'

Chapter Eight

As the Scrap Yard kids walked into the barn, Mercury Boy said, 'This is cool. Draft free with electricity, this can't be bad.' Then looking around, 'what's that over there in the corner?' Looking more closely. 'It looks like two birds. I wonder why they don't fly away?'

Billy Took said, 'they've been stuffed.'

Mercury boy asked, 'who by?'

'I don't know. Probably a taxidermist.'

'Is a taxidermist anything like a taxi driver?'

'No, a taxidermist stuffs birds and animals so shut up otherwise I will get you stuffed.'

'Well, what do they stuff them with?' asked Mercury Boy.

'Bits of straw, cotton wool, sticks, bits of twigs polystyrene anything that they can lay their hands on.'

'Let me tell you, I am not sleeping over there with those birds. I might wake up in the night and find I have been stuffed with cotton wool bit of twigs straw, and polystyrene. Mummies in ancient Egypt thousands of years ago used to get stuffed,' said Mayzack.

'Well I will tell you now, nobody is going to stuff my mum with bits of straw and polystyrene.'

That might not be a bad thing, thought, Copper.

Copper

Copper: Very quiet and careful, he is a safe pair of hands and can be relied on in any situation. He had ambitions to be a doctor but could not stand the sight of blood. His brain is always on full alert. The other three have noticed that on his right side he has a nervous twitch that comes from his mother's side of the family. If you mentioned it to him he is likely to blow a gasket.

Once in the barn with the door closed, it was time to explore. After they had commented on the stuffed birds, they made themselves comfortable. What was on their minds was that, Inspector Nickam. All agreed that it would be madness to get too close to the others and get tarred with the same brush. Can any of you hear that scratching? No came the answer.

'There it is again, listen.'

Mayzack asked, 'When we all came into the barn, I was sure there was an old rusty shovel, propped up against the inside of the door. It's gone now.'

'Well I have not touched it. What about you, Mercury Boy?' Didn't know it was there. That scratching could be those birds trying to get rid of their stuffing. Well, I know if they move, I am out of here.'

Mayzack was the first to close his eyes quickly followed by the other three.

They had been asleep for well over three hours.

Billy Took stirred and then with his eyes open he could hear banging. His first thoughts, was it the birds? Surely those stuffed birds can't play a drum set. It was coming from the barn door. Who the Dickens is that he thought. Once at the door he opened it gingerly and there was standing a very old man. He looked over a hundred years old. His skin was grey and what hair he had had turned snow white.

'Who are you?' asked Billy Took with a surprised expression on his face.

His speech was slurred and quite soft but he eventually said, 'some call me Dicky Rump, others Old Joe, but mostly I am known as, Don't Come Back. I am wondering if you have taken my pipe and matches? They were a present from my Aunt Hilda. Did you know my aunt was a very large lady and she smoked a pipe?'

Standing there looking at the old man, he heard one of the others shout, 'who is it?'

Surprised, Billy Took shouted back, 'some old geezer wants to know if we have got his pipe and matches. I know one thing. He don't half need a wash. He stinks to high heaven. Look come in and tell us where you have come from. We may be able to help you.'

Hobbling across the barn the old man was glad to squat down on a bale of straw, the other three looked at him. Billy Took was right, he didn't half pen and ink.

Mayzack, keeping his distance, was the first to speak.' Have you got any family who live close by? Perhaps your aunt lives up the road?'

Catching his breath, 'Oh yes, I have, let me think. There are ten of us, eleven if you count Billy and Aunt Hilda.'

'Do you know where they live?' asked Mayzack.

'Yes they are not too far from here if I remember correctly. My trouble is I don't know what direction to take.'

'Can you remember their names?' murmured Copper.

The old man sat there thinking, 'no there are too many of us. I do remember Billy though.'

Copper looked at the other three, then at the old man.' Why do you remember Billy?'

'Simple. He has got great big horns,.Well he did have, I am sure he did.'

Billy Took looked flustered. 'Take your time and tell us about the other ten, now think slowly.'

The old man closed his eyes and started to rock from side to side after about two minutes, opening one of his eyes he said, 'yes there is Porky, Best, Chairman, Miss Dorothy, Fat Percy, Gladys, I can't seem to remember the rest. Did I mention Billy the Goat?'

As Mercury Boy had been listening to this, he shouted so loudly 'Billy is a goat.'

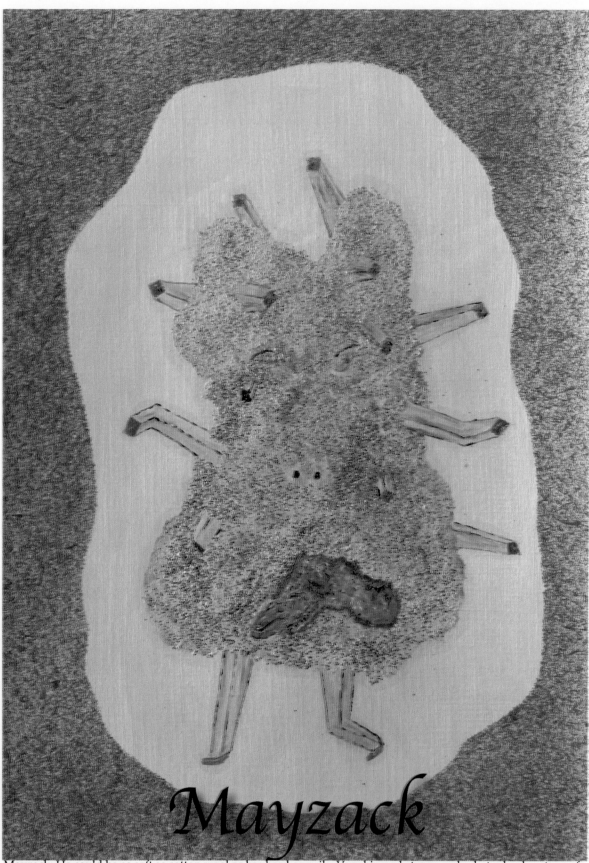

Mayzack

Mayzack: He could be as soft as cotton wool or has hard as nails. Very big and strong, nobody took advantage of him. If his mood took him, he would often do the opposite. He was a very fussy eater, I don't like this, I don't like that. Beans on toast and chicken roll was his favourite. Just don't touch his ice cream. The one member he did not like was Copper. He thought he was greedy and stupid. Copper thought Mayzack was the same.

The old man looked startled.

'Billy's my friend we often play together. Billy is a very good magician and I am his assistant. Porky is a bit grumpy in the morning but Best is ok though. The Pigs are my closest friends, the rest of us are one big family, and all of us chickens get on extremely well.'

The four of them were speechless, they instantly knew he was off his trolley.

'Well then what are we going to do with him?'

'Well, he can't stay here, he might think the stuffed birds are part of his family.'

'We could take him to the hospital,' said Mayzack, 'We could say we found him wandering the streets.'

'Mercury Boy that's not a bad idea, or what about asking a ransom for him.'

Mayzack stared at him. 'You mean kidnap? But he came to us.'

Billy Took said, 'Look over there by the window, we can make him a cup of tea and think about it. By the way, where is, Copper?'

Mercury Boy said, 'I saw him going out for a walk not so long ago.'

Billy Took had something else to ponder. Speaking to the other two he said…

'Do you realise there was not a scrap of rubbish to pick up which means we have no cash coming in and if you want to eat we must do something quick.'

Chapter Nine

The Pope was all of a do-dah. He had promised Honkey and Dorrey that they would have a night watchman called Joe starting immediately. He racked his brains, how am I going to find the old boy Joe? Thinking on his feet, could he get a double or a look alike, with half a brain?

Charlie Parsnip said, 'why not put up posters? Mad night watchman gone missing. Have you seen this bloke? Well, you never know, it's worth a go.'

Thinking hard, The Pope looked up and said, 'that's not a bad idea. Let's forget the word mad, we could offer some of those out of date sausages as a reward, that would get rid of some of them.'

Joey pear laughed. 'Who in their right mind wants sausages that are stuffed with odd ingredients for finding a mad man?'

Listening to this Bok Choy immediately sprang into action.

'Leave the posters to me. There is a chap does all the printing, designing, cash only. I know he will do a rush job, if need be. I will stick the posters everywhere, even places you could not see.'

The Pope once again shook his head in disbelief. To look at a poster in a place where you can't see it?

Copper had sneaked off when the others were talking about stuffed birds pigs and chickens. Wondering around on his own was so peaceful, he forgot all about the time. Wandering along the road from a distance, he could just make out a figure not much taller than two feet in height. Copper had never seen anyone so small and wondered if he had any legs. He seemed to be struggling with three boxes. Copper hid in the tall bushes so that the little person with the boxes would think that there was no one about.

With a swift action, the little person placed the boxes on the ground close to an abandoned building which had a side gate. From where he was hiding, the gate seemed to be slightly open, with no indication of a lock. Next, the little person did two things. One was to look at his watch. With a new

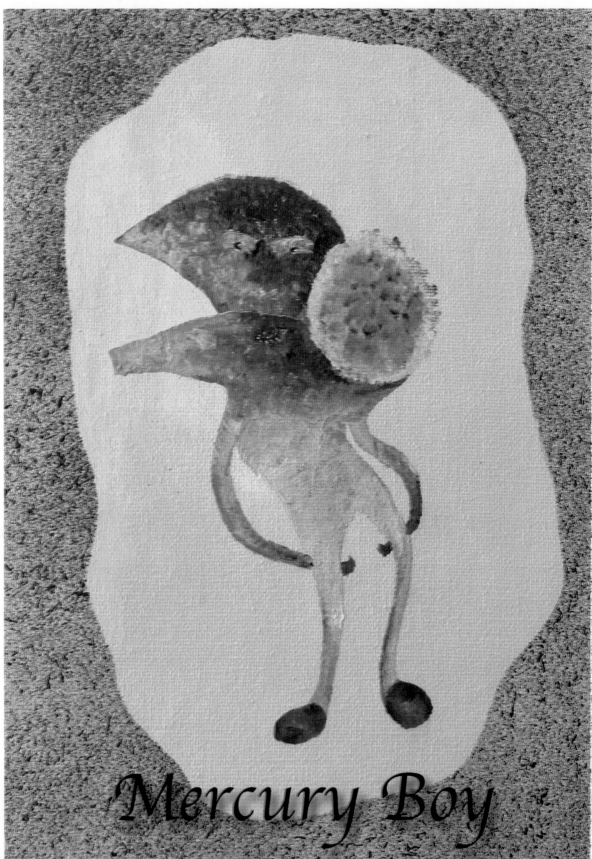

Mercury Boy

Mercury boy: Nobody knew who put boy on the end of his name but he did have a nickname of QS. Everywhere he went or person he spoke to would say, what does QS stand for? He would answer Quick Silver. If you shouted at him he would take offence easily. He was always up for mischief and thought life was one big game. His disability was that he often limped due to five nuts and bolts in his leg. Just don't ask him how they got there. So he was not quick.

battery it worked. The other to look around, seeing nobody about he scarpered back the way he had come as if his life depended on it.

Copper watched and waited. Five minutes went by, then ten and after fifteen minutes he started to become restless. After a while, his curiosity got the better of him. He slid out of the bushes across the road and peeped into the top box. In went his hand and out came a tin of treacle. Doing some quick sums, three boxes of eight that made twenty four tins of this treacle. That may bring in a bob or two.

Now Copper also did two things, one was to have a very good look around and the second was to pick up the boxes and scarper back to the barn without anybody seeing him. The barn door flew open as if it had been blown up. Copper raced through the entrance kicking the door shut with his foot and dropping the boxes down shouting, 'Look what I have found.'

Chapter Ten

The Pope in a pickle

As time went on, The Pope became more agitated and flustered. He had a backup plan but it was a risky one. He went over to Bok Choy speaking quietly, asking him nicely would he do him a favour. Bok Choy looked at The Pope and instantly knew it would be dodgy.

'If you want me to put glue on those used stamps the answer is no.'

Pope went red in the face. 'No, no it's nothing like that.'

'And I am not going to wash the blood off of those bandages or put glue on those used sticky plasters. You can get someone else to do that,' Bok Choy shouted.

'If you want to replace those labels on those tins, or change the sell by date on the mike cartons, get one of the others to do it.'

'This job is a piece of cake, Look I am in a bit of a pickle. Would you for one night be a night watchman on a sausage factory? I will pay you well, top dollar honest. All you have got to do is wander around and twiddle your thumbs, please just for me. I wanted your uncle to do it but now he has gone walkabout.'

Bok Choy looked at the Pope and smiled, 'Yes for you, I just hope this is not one of your scams that you are pulling, if it goes wrong I am in the soup and I can't swim.'

Back in the barn.

Billy Took stood looking at the tins, then said, 'well done. That is just what we need. Now think how is the best way to turn these little darlings into cash. Look I am going to wander over to the old man and have another chat with him.'

The old man was still half asleep as Billy Took sat down beside him, giving him a gentle dig in the ribs.

'I think it is time to return home, I am sure you will be missed. Now I will go and open the barn door and see you on your way.'

As he struggled to his feet the old man ambled over to the door, nodded to Billy Took and started to walk away. As quick as a flash Billy Took said to Mayzack, 'follow him see where he goes, and don't let him out of your sight.'

Nodding he said, 'I am on my way'.

Sam Honkey

Sam Honkey had known his mate many years. They might have met when they were both in prison. He was crafty and thrifty with money and was known to have his fingers into lots of different things some profitable. Others were a total secret. He was well-dressed but spoke with a cockney accent.

The old man stumbled about and crossed the road without a thought to see what was coming, but seemed not to know where he was going. He then plonked himself down on the ground for a minute or two and then he heaved himself up and staggered on until finally, he stopped at a large dilapidated house. Why would anybody want to look at a house that was fit for demolition? Maybe he was looking to squat. Climbing the steps he banged on the old front door to which there was no answer. This time he banged harder making more of the paint, that was flaking, come off. The door bell lay on the top step and both wires were hanging loose.

The door was open by Miss Tinsnap, her face showing real anger. She was going to close it quickly but then thought better of it. She began shouting, 'now clear off and don't come back. If you do I will call the police and have you arrested.'

Blowing his cheeks out he bellowed at Miss Tinsnap, 'I am the police.'

She then started to cough softly at first then louder and louder.

He had no idea what to do as his training as meteorologist did not include a coughing fit. Trying to get his words out he finally said, 'If I can use your phone I will call a doctor. Did you know that before I was a police officer, I trained as a doctor and I would recommend that you get that cough looked at. You may need a chest x ray along with some jollop.'

The coughing eventually stopped. She regained her breath and said, 'I have called the police. You need locking up. You're a menace to the general public. One minute you are a chicken, then you are a police officer and now a trained doctor. Was that before or after you were a meteorologist?'

With that, the door was slammed shut making more loose paint fall on the steps. He kicked the doorbell into the undergrowth, avoiding the bear wires. By chance he looked up, making sure that no roof tiles had become loose.

He stood looking up at his old home wondering why he could not have his own room back. If the bombs start to fall he would be glad to go in the cupboard under the stairs and I won't light my pipe. Promise. He knew Miss Tinsnap was hiding behind the nicotine stained curtains that were twitching probably puffing on her pipe.

From behind him, a voice said, 'Sir can you give me your name?'

Turning around was a man in a blue suit, fairly smart, quite young and standing beside a police car that was parked at the side of the road.

'If you don't mind me asking what are you up to, are you impersonating a police officer, there is a lot of that about you know. Your name sir?'

'What name do you want?'

'Well, how many have you got?'

'Three I think or is it four?'

'Just give me all of them.'

'Dicky Rump, Old Joe, and Don't come back.'

'Okay, now where have you just come from?'

Let me think, 'Err an old barn, I am sure it was an old barn, or maybe a stately home.'

'Where is this barn or stately home?'

'Sorry I have no idea.'

'Could you please tell me what you are doing standing outside this big old house?'

'I am waiting to see if it all falls down. If it does I intend to rush in, well perhaps not rush, grab my pipe and matches from old what's her name. I used to live here. Miss Tinsnap won't let me in, I am

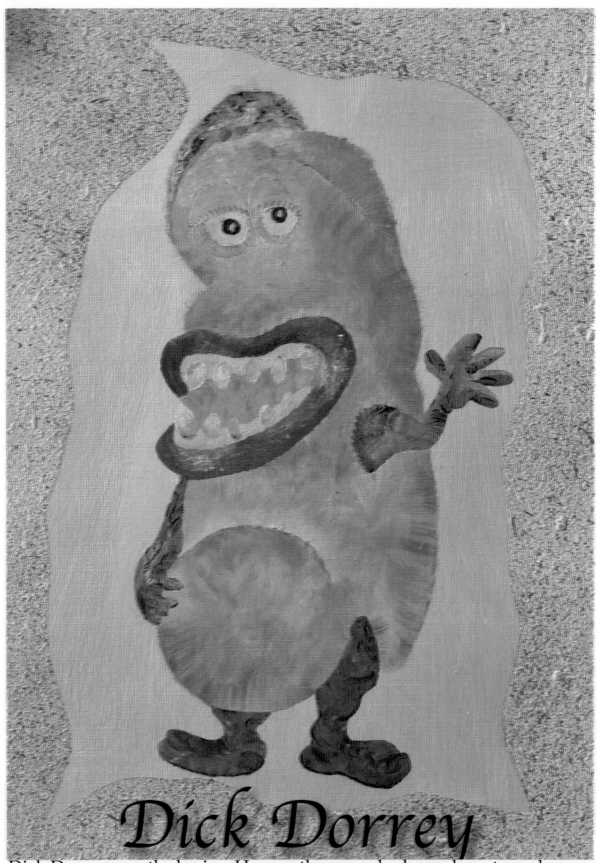

Dick Dorrey

Dick Dorrey was the brains. He was the one who knew how to make money. He had been well educated but took life a little too seriously. Hee had a very short fuse and could blow up at the least little thing.

barred, she has taken my pipe and matches away. Did you know there was a fire here? It was only a little one, honest.'

'Let's move on. Was there anyone in the barn with you?'

'Are to talking about the fire?'

'What fire?'

'The one you have just mentioned.'

'I didn't say there was a fire in the barn. In the bedroom, yes.'

'No, yes, there were four of them. They weren't police officers or doctors and did I mention two birds that were there locked in a cage.'

'So you were in a barn with four others, and two birds locked in a cage, but there was no fire at that time?'

'Fire in the bedroom? It was only a little one.'

'So why are you repeating everything I say?'

'What are the names of these others?'

'You don't half ask difficult questions. If you had asked me say eighty years ago, I may have been able to tell you but today I don't know what day it is. Sometimes I struggle to remember my own name.'

'Okay, come with me. Inspector Nickam will get to the bottom of this.'

As he led him to his patrol car, Old Joe said, 'I can't get into your car, I don't even know who you are. You have got to be so careful today. You could be impersonating a police officer and abducting me.'

'Sir, I would be glad to show you my warrant card if it makes you feel more at ease.'

'No that won't be necessary, but don't drive too fast, I get car sickness. Well, I used to fifty years ago.'

Chapter Eleven

The Sausage Factory

Bok Choy half turned and looked directly at The Pope as they walked to the factory. He had a feeling of sickness in his stomach, that things were not going to go smoothly. Once they were there Sam was waiting for them and immediately started giving Bok Choy the do's and don'ts along with safety instructions. Before he reached the factory he had said to, The Pope, 'this job as a night watchman, if it is at night I won't be able to see.'

'Yes you will. Sam will give you a torch, and you will be ok.'

'If I am hungry can I pop out and get some chips?'

'No, you can't, if you are hungry eat some of those sausages that are inside.'

'Will there be any mustard there?'

'No.'

'But you know I am not keen on sausages, with or without mustard. I prefer a nice steak pie.'

'You can have a pie tomorrow, just wander around twiddle your thumbs and make sure nobody steals the sausages. It's as simple as that.'

After the safety instructions, Sam led Bok Choy into the factory leaving The Pope to return home, thinking I do hope that it goes smoothly.

In the Police station

41

Inspector Nickam

Inspector Nickham was a devoted policeman. He enjoyed nothing better than sending criminals to prison. Recently he had been promoted to the elite frying pan squad. Being tough he took no back chat from anyone. Sometimes little things got him down. After many years of service he thought about retirement and doing his large garden.

The old man with three names was led into a tiny room with just two chairs and a table that was bolted to the floor. He was told to sit down and be quiet.

Ten minutes went by and then Inspector Nickam walked in, sat down and started to open a file in front of him. 'First, your name' he asked as he shuffled his papers.

The old man looked at the inspector but said nothing.

Nickam's face was tight with anger, shouting, 'I have asked you a question, answer me.'

The old man eventually said, 'I was told to be quiet, now you want me to talk, I wish you would make up your mind.'

'Yes, yes, I know all about that, just tell me your name.'

'Eh.. Dicky Rump or Old Joe or Don't Come Back. I can't think of any more, there may be more.'

'Right, how old are you?'

Old Joe thought about the question for about three or four minutes.

'I really don't know, but I do remember being about ten, there was a girl in my class at school called, what's her name, thingumy bob? I will be with you in a minute or two. Jean? Jenny? Julie? Nice looking girl with brown eyes. Now I know how old she was, about ten. Well she would be if she was in the same class. Have you seen her Mr Nickam? I hope she is not in any sort of trouble.'

'Look,' said Nickam, 'forget the girl for the moment. I know all about your mates and the two birds that are in a cage.'

'Those birds in the cage are not the ones I went to school with. I am sure of it. Birds in a cage. You sure Mr Nickam? Not one of them birds that was in my class at school? If they were chickens they could be part of my family. Don't get too rough with them will you, and they are not to be eaten or to say the word stuffing.'

'Okay, forget the chickens and the birds, they will not be mentioned again.'

'Also it is a very serious offence to impersonate a police officer. Do you understand what I am saying to you?'

'Are you saying that these chickens have been impersonating police officers? You are making this up.'

Nickam thought, now how long before I retire?

Then Old Joe, thought about it and then said, 'It was not me, it was, Dicky Rump.'

Nickam looked a little lost. 'You now are saying Dicky Rump is a police officer?'

'Yes, Mr Nickam. Dicky Rump is a ventriloquist as well as a police officer and a very good one at that.'

Nickam got up from his chair, picked up his papers, and went out slamming the door shut. Mumbling to himself, he isn't all the ticket. He made his way down to his office and sat at his desk, trying to calm down.

Nickam shouted, 'Sergeant Stickit? Come in here. I have got this old lunatic here. I want both of us to try and get his age and maybe get his fingerprints. Also to tell us where the barn is, and any other intelligent information that he has got.'

'Before we go to see him, I have had a lot of reports of stolen clothes clothes from washing lines. Look I know you have a lot on your plate, cast your eyes over these reports. The clothes are not worth much but they may fetch a pound or two down the market, I would not put it beyond this lot to have their grubby hands involved. Lets go.'

As they both walked into the room, Old Joe was fast asleep. Stickit bellowed, 'Get your arms off the table now. I want you to tell us where he barn is.'

Old Joe was startled by the shouting, as he looked at the pair of them. Opening his mouth he said,' so

Daisy

Daisy is a tiny and beautiful yellow flower with a smokey and dark sort of voice. She was the first to talk to Lilian and has the biggest smile in the garden. Her bestest, bestest friend is Delion. Both are not that friendly with Entwistle. If the sun is shining she gets on her cart and flies around the garden on it.

you have found my pipe and matches? Where were they? I have looked everywhere for them. I bet Miss Tin something or other, whatever her name is has had my pipe.'

'Ok you can have your pipe and matches back,' Stickit said, 'but first, where is the barn? And one other thing. Those clothes that you have on where did they come from? They look a little small for you. Looking at the quality , I am not sure that they are your style.'

'Style? What style, I will let you know I have been a very snappy dresser in my time. After the war, my dress code was like the bee's knees. Smart straight lines and slim fit. Not like the old clothes that you lot have got on today.'

Sitting there thinking, finally Joe said, 'Look you have my pipe and matches, if you think you can take away my clothes, you have another think coming. I remember buying these, it was just after the war. Now was it the First or the Second? Just give me a minute or two. I will have to ask Dicky Rump. He knows I am just the ventriloquist.'

At that moment there was a loud knock on the door.

'An urgent call for you inspector.'

As he went out of the door, he muttered, 'Nothing is easy today.'

Chapter Twelve

Back home

All three had slept very well, only Joey Pear was still asleep. The Pope, as he opened his eyes somehow felt something was wrong. He was sure of it, but could not put his finger on it. There was a nagging feeling at the back of his brain. It did not take long for that feeling to come true.

With blue lights flashing, he knew something was not good to see two police vehicles, one of them a van. A shiver of fear went down his spine. Charlie Parsnip thought he would make a run for it, but deep down he could not leave the other two.

Bang Bang went to the door knocker of Toadstool's house. The Pope tried to wake Joey Pear shouting through the letterbox, 'get up, get up, the police are here.'

'I am coming, hold your horses.'

Joey Pear opened the front door and looking at, Inspector Nickam, she went as white as a sheet. Standing there in her nightdress, with no slippers on and no teeth.

Nickam bellowed,' Pope in the car, you two in the van.'

'We ain't done nuffin honest. We have been asleep all night,' murmured Joey Pear. 'Have I got time for a cup of tea?'

'No, put some clothes on and get a move on.'

Nickam looked at the three of them with a big smile on his face.

'That's so, well tell me how the sausage factory has had all the sausages stolen and the place is burning out of control. Get a move on you three.'

Delion

Delion is a dainty flower, She is not very tall and she has a big round bright yellow face. She laughs and giggles at the least little thing. One minuet she pops up gone the next, where to no one knows, then pops up again. Can often be seen with Daisy telling each other jokes. She loves her green wellies.

Chapter Thirteen

Back in the police station

Bok Choy sat on a hard most uncomfortable bench. He had been told not to move and not to ask any questions. His throat was red raw due to the volume of smoke from the fire. He asked to see a doctor but was told 'shut it'. His clothes were covered in soot. Sitting there for over three hours his thoughts drifted back to Icicles Island. It was cold but it was a more simple way of life.

Walking towards Bok Choy, half dragging and half pulling Old Joe along the hallway, was Stickit. When Bok Choy saw Joe. He jumped to his feet shouting, 'Uncle Joe Uncle Joe,' who instantly recognized Bok Choy and shouted back, 'Thank goodness. It's good to see you.'

They both said the same thing.

'What are you doing in here?' Joe spoke first, 'This place is like a mad house, they have pinched my pipe, now they want my clothes. There are some in here that are impersonating chickens. Can you believe that? And Dicky Rump somewhere in here being a ventriloquist.'

Stickit looked at them both. 'Do you know this bloke?'

'Yes, yes he is my uncle on my mother's side. What is he doing here?'

Stickit said nothing. He just stared at them both.

Joe answered, 'I don't know, there is an Inspector somewhere in here. Did you know he is related to Dicky Rump who is also a ventriloquist? He has also got my pipe and matches and won't give them back.'

Stickit immediately put old Joe in a room, locking the door then he flew down a flight of stairs, shot into the Inspector's office puffing and panting.

'You won't believe this, that mad old fool is related to one of the Dead End Gang. The one they call Bok Choy.'

Nickam smiled. 'finally a breakthrough, all is not lost, get that Bok Choy character into room two now.'

'Already done.'

Bok Choy was pushed into a small room with just a table and two chairs.

'I want a cup of tea, and where is the doctor? I know my rights in here,' he said.

'You have no rights in here, sunshine. Another thing, what have you lot done with the washing that's been borrowed/nicked? Probably sold down the market.'

'Washing? What washing', we ain't taken no washing down the market. We have taken TVs, washing machines, fridge freezers, electric tooth brushes, toasters. Once we took down the market an old gearbox that came from an old Ford Escort. A 1979 model, I think. It was in good condition except that for some reason the oil kept running out of the bottom. It didn't sell, so we dumped it. But no washing.'

'So, you got me there, Inspector. Washing? As I said, us lads don't touch washing. We leave all that to the ladies.'

The door was slammed shut, leaving him on his own again.

Nickam and Stickit moved down the passageway in long strides, then took the stairs two at a time. When they reached the door, Stickit half pushed and half kicked, making the door fly open and giving Bok Choy a shock. One stood and one sat down.

'Now before we start this interview,' Nickam said,' I want to know where this barn is, that your uncle

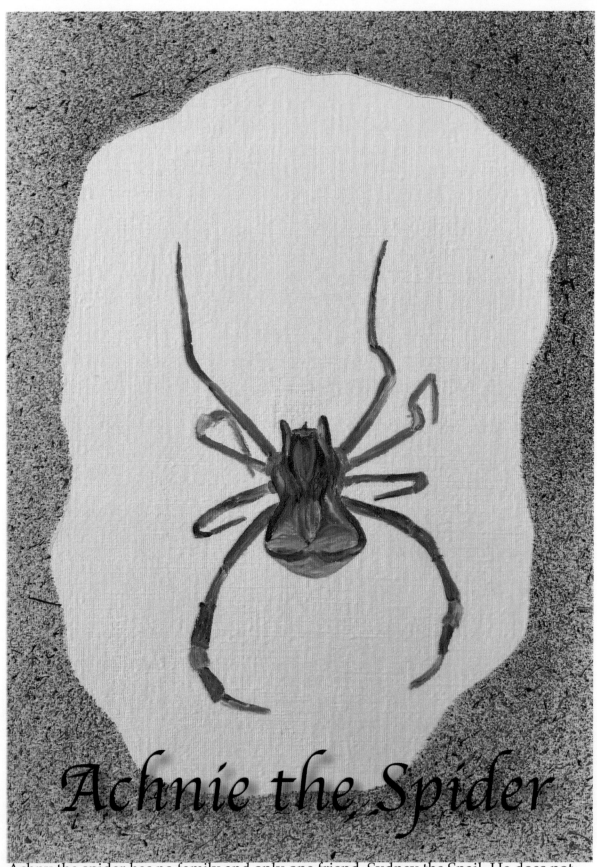

Achnie the Spider

Achny the spider has no family and only one friend, Sydney the Snail. He does not have a lot of money so he can't pay any rent. Did find him a nice place. It was dry, clean and no noisy neighbours. The only thing Achny did not like was the smell of coffee from the cafe up the road.

stayed in. If you don't cooperate you won't be leaving here. You will never see the light of day again, do you understand me?'

'Loud and clear. Yes, could I have a cup of tea? I am so thirsty. It may even help to loosen my tongue. Two sugars and two biscuits could help.'

Nickam asked, 'Where is the barn? Then you can have tea.'

'Look I am telling you the truth. I don't know it all. I know it's not far from the old people's home that my uncle stayed in. It's along the street through the tunnel, turn left, or is it right? I am not too sure. There was an old barn that lies back off the road. We used to store some rubbish in there. Well not exactly rubbish, just stuff that happens to lay around, if you know what I mean. It could be that one. It's the only one I know. Now can I have tea? Can I see a doctor now?' said Bok Choy. 'Being in this place gives me frightful headaches. Do you get headaches in here, Mr Nickam?'

'Normally no, but I do with you lot in here!'

Nickam and Stickit went out slamming the door shut without saying a word. They heard him screaming, 'you can't do this to me. What happens if I die of thirst? Or my head goes bang from this headache?'

Nickam spoke, 'get two cars round to that barn and bring in whoever is in there, including the birds in a cage. Break the locks if you have to, don't let anybody get away. If you spot anything that looks dodgy, that could be used as evidence, bag and number it, got it? I also think you should call the bomb squad and have the fire brigade on standby. Gunpowder makes me come out all sweaty. Don't turn on any lights in the barn, if there is a spark, with gunpowder in there.'

Stickit nodded turned and moved like greased lightning.

Chapter Fourteen

Taking it easy

Three of the scrap yard kids wanted a cooked breakfast in a café just up the road from the police station. Two of them wondered where the old man was, wandering the streets alone not knowing what day it was, but their main topic of conversation was how to get some money. Some of the ideas were a bit dangerous, silly and very risky. It was agreed that they would go back to the barn have a brew and then, split up into pairs. That way they could cover twice as much ground.

Billy Took said, 'First let's get rid of those tins of treacle. They may fetch a bob or two.' Mayzack had overheard that there was some bloke selling bars of soap. Not cheap but the flavour and smell was quite unique. He could be contacted and an offer put to him. It is worth a try.'

'Not a bad idea, let's start there.'

Sipping their tea they could hear the squealing of tyres. They knew there was a race track not far away, but this was right outside the barn. Copper froze and then said, 'who the Dickens is that?'

Just at that moment, the barn door burst open and what seemed like an army of police officers came rushing through the door ready to arrest anybody.

Stickit shouted, 'Police' as if nobody knew who they were.

'Don't move a muscle. Hands on your heads'. Nobody moved. Again Stickit shouted, 'Hands on your heads' still, nobody moved.

Mercury Boy speaking quietly,' If we put our hands on our heads, our muscles will have to move.'

Sidney the Snail

Sidney the snail is liked by others for his coolness but he is also the slowest snail in the world. It takes Sidney ten minutes to turn around. Achny the spider is his closest friend. Sometimes they sit around all day just talking a load of rubbish and what they fancied for dinner that evening.

Stickit smiled at Mercury Boy. 'So we have a joker in the pack, you won't be joking when we are through with you lot, I can assure you.'

With a quiet voice Billy Took said, 'You are interrupting us having our morning cuppa and biscuits. What have we supposed to have done?'

'Done?' said Stickit. 'Kidnap, imprisonment handling stolen goods, destruction of property, resisting arrest, I might throw in murder just for good measure. Now which one of you is going to tell me where the two birds are being kept against their will.'

It was at that moment, all four started to laugh. Once they got the giggles they couldn't stop. Mayzack looked at the police, who wondered why they were laughing uncontrollably.

'You lot think we have kidnapped two birds and put them in a cage, holding them against their will?'

Still bent over double with shrieks of laughter, Copper who could not keep a straight face, pointed to the two stuffed birds that were in a cage. Even some of the police now had a smile on their faces.

Stickit was red in the face, shouted, 'get those four down the nick, along with any evidence right now.'

They were manhandled out of the barn door into waiting police cars, ready for the short ride to the station. Nobody gave a thought to shut the barn door, passing the café where only one hour ago they had enjoyed their cooked breakfast.

Chapter Fifteen

Back in the Police station

Old Joe was pacing up and down, in a tiny room on his own. Mumbling, I want a cup of tea and give me my pipe and baccy back. He was now shouting but nobody was listening. 'You can have my shirt and trousers if you want. Just give me my pipe back.' If they did nobody was taking a blind bit of notice.

Sitting at his desk with a very large smile on his face, inspector Nickam shouted, 'someone bring me a mug of tea.' His thoughts were what the Chief Inspector would say. Just then a PC arrived with his mug of tea. Stickit walked in and sat.

'I have got the old bloke in room one, Dippy in another, his three mates in room four, and the other four downstairs in room seven. Where do you want me to start, gov?'

'Right get someone to get all their names and addresses, dates of birth, where they come from and any other information that may be of use.'

Stickit nodded, 'I am on it.'

There was a knock at the door, the PC said, 'sorry but there are two blokes downstairs, a Sam Honkey and Dick Dorrey. They are jumping up and down and going mad, they are the owners of the sausage factory and are demanding blood.'

'Put them in a room and give them a cup of tea, 'Stickit said. 'And some biscuits. Try to soften them up a bit.'

Nickam was at his desk working on a plan to get the best results, it must have been about thirty minutes, then the PC knocked on the door again.

'Sorry there are five more in reception. One has had his warehouse broken into and a quantity of bars of soap taken. There is a Mr. Stinker who owns the fish shop, The Pope sold him a quantity of winkles that have resulted in eight people getting food poisoning. Then there is a miniature person that claims to have had his tins of treacle stolen and two men, one the owner, and one technician. Their laboratory

Sargeant Stickit

Sargeant Stickit by name, stick it by nature. Everybody wondered how Stickit ever got in to the police force. He was at times vague and forgetful but also funny at times. One thing he hated was filling in paperwork. He was best having a cup of tea in a cafe getting to know the local villains.

has had twenty sets of false teeth go missing plus about twelve people shouting and screaming, wondering if they are going to get their washing back and who took their clothes.'

Nickam said,' thank you please close the door.' In the quietness of his office he thought, this is going to be a tricky one to put all this together, I think I will start with Bok Choy. He is likely to crack first, and give us some insight into the goings on.'

Nickam opened the door, just as Stickit came into view.

'Come with me. We will do Bok Choy first. Let's start softly, softly and then build on that. If nothing works, tell him he is going away for life.'

Bok Choy looked tired and as white as a sheet. He was standing up as his legs were aching. The door flew open Nickam said, 'sit down, Stickit,' pointing to a chair.

'First I want you to tell me how you got the job at the factory, what time did you start, everything you know up until the fire started, and don't make anything up, otherwise you will never see daylight again, do you understand? If you do just nod.'

Bok Choy nodded two or three times.

'The Pope got me the job, I didn't want to do it, honest. I don't like sausages, I prefer a meat pie. When I was in the factory on my own, I became frightened. I could hear all sorts of noises and then things started to move on their own. The lights started to flicker, then my stomach told me I was hungry, so I popped out to get some chips. A bit expensive but they were not greasy. I even thought about a bit of fish, but with the cost of the chips, I settled for a meat pie. Those sausages tasted terrible. Rhubarb and cough mixture flavour, is disgusting. I could not find any red or brown sauce and no mustard either. How do they expect people to eat that muck without sauce or mustard? Do you like sauce, Mr Nickam? I bet you like mustard, Mr Stickit, 'said Bok Choy.

Nickam screamed, 'just get on with it and leave the pie, sauce and mustard out.'

Bok Choy nodded again. 'But I think it is an important part of the story. After about two hours or was it three? I am not quite sure, my eyes started to close. I think it was because my belly was quite full after steak pie and chips. I tried but I could not keep them open and I must have drifted off. How long I was asleep for I have no way of knowing. I have a watch. Look it's a good one, the thing is it doesn't work. Now where was I. Ah yes, asleep, I must have been dreaming, here I was on a tropical beach, blue sea and sky, palm trees the works. A little breeze coming off the ocean, I was thinking of lunch. Grilled chicken and a cold beer.'

Nickam this time bellowed, 'get off the beach and get back into the factory.'

'Okay, okay, now where was I? Yes, asleep. The smell of those stinking sausages along with the black smoke gave me quite a fright, I can tell you. It was dark with all that smoke and I couldn't find my torch I had no idea what the time was. You do know that my watch does not work anyway, I made my way to the top of the stairs, finally, I ended up outside which was a damn good thing because I may have got burnt like those sausages. Then I would not be able to tell you about the sauce and the mustard and the tropical beach, with the chicken for lunch.'

'Don't stop, keep going, what happened next?'

'Let me think, don't rush me for a minute or two. Nothing. My eyes were stinging from the smoke. You do know there was a lot of black smoke. You do know that black smoke is not good for your lungs. Once that black stuff goes into you it won't come out. Some people have had to have new lungs. You ain't got new lungs, have you, Mr Nickam? I noticed that the door was open and the place was filling up with thick black smoke. Well, it would do if there was a fire. Now I happened to notice three or was

Chief Inspector Doug Greengage

Chief Inspector Doug Greengage was known in the police station as an old likeable man. Slim he had a cocky attitude to life. If he could sneak off either to home or the pub he was gone. Although when he put his mind to a problem he would solve it even if it took him all week.

it four figures climbing over the fence. Then they disappeared down the lane by the side of the factory. I thought did the smoke get into their eyes and down into their lungs.?If it did, will they be wanting new lungs?'

Stickit immediately wanted to know if you see them again. 'Could you identify them?'

'It was dark with all that smoke, I don't think so but I am sure they were all female.' Bok Choy went on to explain that one of them looked maybe familiar.

'It was the last one, she sort of turned and looked back. I did wonder if she was the one that reads the news in the evening on the TV, you know the one, red hair and big teeth. Mind you when she looked back, she did have some sort of mask on.'

Stickit looked at Nickam, and both thought the same. Bok Choy is not all the ticket, just like the old man, his uncle.

Slamming the door shut, the last they heard as they walked away was, 'can I have a cup of tea, and what about a doctor? Don't forget I have rights. I demand to see a solicitor.'

'What about those four from the barn? Let's give them a good grilling,' Stickit said as they both walked down the stairs. Nickam thought for a minute.

'Get someone to take a statement, from the two that own the sausage factory. Also the fishmonger chap and the one that lost tins of treacle. Then there's the man with the soap and don't forget those two from the laboratory. Right, meet me outside room seven.'

Two of the Scrapyard kids were pacing up and down, like nervous wrecks. The other two sat still staring at the floor.

Billy Took said,' we know nothing, right? Don't own up to anything, just sit tight.'

With a loud bang in walked Inspector Nickam and Sergeant Stickit.

'Sit down you lot and first tell me about the fire.'

All four of them looked at each other. Mercury Boy spoke quietly,' What fire? Are you talking about the fire in June 1864?'

'1864 the great fire? What sort of turnip do you take me for? You lot are not doing yourselves any favours.'

Nickam laughed. 'What have you done with the sausages that you stole? You lot could not have knocked them out that quickly, or have eaten them. We found the treacle in the barn and have looked but not yet found the bars of soap or any gunpowder yet, but we will.'

Billy Took coughed and laughed. 'We ain't got no sausages and as for the tins of treacle, they have always been in the barn. As for the soap, we don't use soap, only because we don't wash. Where we come from it's that cold we would freeze to death, if we took our clothes off. Mayzack, tell these two why we don't eat sausages. Where we lived the trees had stopped growing due to the cold, no wood, no fire. We don't eat raw sausages. You could end up with your stomach on fire. Surely you two should know that, and as for gunpowder, forget it, dangerous stuff that. Do you know that you could get your arms and legs blown off? My mate had some gunpowder once, it went off accidentally, blowing a hole in his head. He was never the same again.'

Nickam had a face like thunder.

'What about the greenhouse that was smashed to smithereens? We know you were responsible for that, we have a witness. An old lady, who had just had her eyes tested, saw you running away, one of you was actually hobbling. Which one was it?'

Commander Kale Shoebag

Commander Kale Shoebag was a mean man, slightly pudgy and looked older than sixty years. Behind his back there were lots of names he was known as if you looked at him the wrong way or questioned his authority. Your career could be cut short. Nobody had seen or heard of Mrs Shoebag. Maybe she left him years ago.

Copper spoke up. 'It could not have been us. We were five or six miles away on that day, in the barbers. Sorry, the Cranfield Road hairdressing salon.'

Mercury Boy quickly said, 'no it's two witnesses if you include that fat bloke who got stuck in the chair. I think he had short back and sides. So, we have a witness to prove it.'

Slamming the door the policemen both stood outside in silence for a minute or two. Nickam spoke quite softly.

'Six down, three to go, let's make our way to room four upstairs, this could be our last chance,' Stickit mumbled. 'Have we got all the paperwork, and is it in order?'

Nickam nodded. 'Two of them in room four were asleep. Only The Pope was awake when they walked in. First to speak was, The Pope. 'You cannot keep us locked up in here with nothing to drink, it's inhumane. It must be against our human rights for something.'

Nickam then said, 'I will tell you what is inhumane, having to deal with you, Pope, you have now caused good folk to get food poisoning with those winkles. Then you put Bok Choy in a factory that he did not want to be in. He had no training, so when the fire started he hadn't a clue what to do.'

Looking at the two of them The Pope said, 'I did not sell the winkles to Mr Stinker the fish man I gave them to him. He puts them out for the birds in the garden. The birds like pecking at the winkles, did you know that? I like to help out any way that I can in the community. Honest and reliable are us. As for Bok Choy he was doing Hunky Dory a favour. I didn't want him to go, I tried to stop him, but he said he didn't want to let them down. He didn't know who took the sausages or who started the fire, in my experience as a qualified electrical engineer, an electrical short circuit, probably from a spark that may happen.'

Nickam looked at, The Pope, 'Your experience? What experience? I wouldn't trust you with a blunt knife and a loaf of bread.'

'I think that is a bit unfair, Mr. Nickam. We are pillars of the community, as I have said, hard working lads we are. We go about our business, doing good in the community.'

'Shut it, you will have me in tears in a minute. What about the cheese that has gone missing? Don't tell me you know nothing about it because I know you do.'

The Pope looked cross. We don't know nuffink about cheese, I don't eat the stuff because my skin comes out in big red spots.'

Joey Pear said that, 'the cheese, which has gone mouldy won't do you any good. We wouldn't give it to the birds in the garden.'

Charlie Parsnip commented, 'we did have some cheese some time ago, goat's cheese I think or was it Buffalo cheese, do you know the difference between goat and buffalo cheese, Mr. Nickam?'

'No,' shouted, Nickam, 'but what I do know is that you sold false teeth and you cannot deny it.'

Two of them said at once, 'we did sell false teeth, the profit margin was very small. We bought them at a scout's jumble sale. We knew there was no money in it but we like to help out in the community Mr Nickam.'

'Help the community? You lot would sell your own grandmother if you could.'

'What about the clothes that you have nicked? Probably sold down the market.

'That is an outrageous accusation Mr Nickam. To take hard working people's clothes off their washing line? Whoever does that wants their fingers chopped off. It is a disgraceful thing to do. Once again I think you are being a bit harsh, Mr Nickam. As I said before, we are an honest bunch of hard working lads, trying to get by.'

'The only bye I would like to see is bye-bye to you lot. We will be back so don't think we have gone soft on you.'

As they both walked down the corridor, coming the other way was the Chief Inspector Doug Greengage. Better known in the Station as, Old Age.

'Both of you in my office now.'

Once they were all seated, with the door shut, the Chief Inspector spoke slowly, 'I have read all the reports, it's not looking good. Two gangs of four, an old man who can't remember his name or what day it is. First, there is demolition, destruction of the greenhouse with an unreliable witness. Then those tins of treacle that went missing all of it two years out of date. False teeth bought from a scout's jumble sale. That's not a crime. A load of smelly winkles that were meant for the birds in the garden. Then two birds locked in a cage against their will, I am sure they would have loved to have flown away if the taxidermist had not got there first. Smelly bars of luxury soap, that no one has ever seen or smelt. Then there is the case of the missing cheese, who stole it, nobody knows, nobody wants it because nobody eats it. Then we have the theft of the sausages plus the fire at the factory. I have looked into those two characters, Sam Honkey and Dick Dorrey, a right pair of dodgy misfits. Those missing clothes from washing lines? Hardly a crime of the month. My suggestion would be get all eight of them in one of our vans, drive down to the port, put them on the first ship or ferry to France or Holland and let them deal with them.'

Stickit asked the Chief Inspector,' what shall we do with the old man?'

Giving it some thought. 'Just let him go. On second thoughts, take him round to the council offices, buy him a pipe and matches on the way, and let them deal with him. You never know they may need a completely mad night watchman.'

Just then all three burst out laughing.

The chief inspector Doug Greengage, had his oversized shoes up on the desk. His shirt sleeves rolled up, tie skew-whiff.

He was a simple man, with colourful smile. He certainly knew how to play the system. Some say he invented it. Nickam and Stickit slouched in chairs the other side of his desk. All three looked and felt drained. The strain was there to see.

They were still doubled up with laughter over the old man working for the council, but before the three of them could control themselves, Greengage's office door flew open with the force of a small bomb. Shaking the partition walls causing pictures to fly off of their fixings. It was obvious to all three that the door had been kicked in with tremendous force. Standing there with a face like thunder, his body stiff as a board, was Commander Carl Shoebag. A podgy man who looked older than his sixty years. He screamed, 'so you lot think it's funny do you?'

Greengage's shoes slipped off of the desk and in unison they all stood to attention, like frightened mice, unable to speak. You could cut the tension with a knife. As Shoebag bellowed again, 'laughing you lot? You won't be laughing if I have my way. You lot will be directing traffic for the rest of your days. Now sit!'

It was like looking at three men condemned to a firing squad. With pale faces the commander continued to stand, not that there a chair spare. What was most unusual was the quietness of the station. You could hear a pin drop. A female PC looked in to ask, 'who wants tea?' She got told, 'not now.'

Commander Shoebag broke the silence. 'Which one of you dopey lot tipped off the press?'

From under his arm he produced the latest local paper. Showing, in his opinion, the cruellest of headlines. Two local gangs running wild controlled by Mr Big, alias Dickie Rump, Old Joe or Don't come back. Shouting, 'you couldn't make this up! What were you lot thinking? If you have any brains where are they?'

Inspector Nickam looked at Shoebag, showing real fear in his eyes. Speaking slowly and precisely he said, 'These were very complicated cases which required diplomacy and integrity. It's our policy never to speak to the press without authorisation.' He wondered, have I done enough to dampen the flames, as he looked at Greengage's open mouth hoping he would confirm what he had just said. But nothing came out.

Shoebag's voice seemed quieter but still had venom in it. Glancing at Nickam he said, 'now you lot, I have had the PM on the phone, the Home Office, Boarder Force, and the Intelligent agency, who inform me that the eight are now downstairs in the cells. So if the laughing has ceased, in the next four hours use whatever method you choose. I want them finger printed, full details taken, date of birth etc. Are there any international arrest warrants outstanding? And I want you all back in my office in four hours time. So just get shot of them.'

Stickit, who thought he was better keeping his mouth shut, jumped as Commander Shoebag began galvanising the station into action. Phones began ringing, officers appeared with pieces of paper, everybody was on full alert. Shoebag had promised the nine who were being held downstairs, tea and sandwiches. Pipe and matches for, Mr Big if they fully co-operated, blood would be taken, figure prints collected and a full family history gathered. The station was now being run like a well oiled machine. The only hiccup came from the nine downstairs. Shoebag failed to say when they would be watered and fed.

It took just over three and a half hours to collect process, store and cross reference the data, which enabled the officers to bring this very ugly situation to a swift conclusion.

Inspector Nickam roamed around the station like a headless chicken. In one office and out of another, looking for, Chief Inspector Greengage. His thoughts were, is he outside having a smoke? Walking over to the window to look, but lurking in the corner stood, Shoebag and without warning speaking quickly he said, 'you ain't got time to gaze at the sunset. I want everyone in the conference room in fifteen minutes.'

Nickam, clearly having problems getting his words out, finally said, 'sir we need to address the problem of them that are locked up down stairs, as they are extremely close to a full scale riot due to no food or drink yet.'

Commander Shoebag acknowledged the situation and said, 'give them tea and sandwiches and make sure they shut up.'

Gathered around the conference table, Shoebag had a face like thunder. He glared at those who were seated around the table and in a stable voice said, 'so what have we got?' They all seemed to want to speak at the same time. Finally it was established that there were no arrest warrants out for them, but six member of the two gangs are here with no passports. The one we call Mr Big (we cannot establish his true identity) but with a lot of digging we found that he emigrated from Southern Ireland. We have also found that there is a strong possibility that he is related to Bok Choy. Charlie Parsnip is a distant cousin, except we have yet to establish a confirmed link. Both of these have out of date IDs. Records in Southern Ireland are patchy to say the least. There was so much coming and going, half the information is fictitious.

Around the table all eyes were on Shoebag, his word was law. Now not looking at anybody in particular he said, 'I have digested all the information that we have received, our first task is to get rid of the six gang members. It will require two vans to leave tonight. Destination is Hull docks, where you will be met by two undercover detectives, called Bronk and Dover. They will have the necessary paperwork to enter Pen Six for them to board a container ship called Damp Poo. Just get them on that ship. Tell them they are going on a cruise or something. It leaves at 12.15 am our time. Do that and it should be the last we see or hear of them. Got it? The two undercover detectives will remain on board with them until the very last minute.'

Stickit had the same thoughts as Nickam. Surely they just won't let them loose at the first port that the container ship docks at. Nobody has given any thought about personal belongings, money etc.

Carl Shoebag then flipped through is notes, coughed a couple of times but was not looking at anybody in particular.

'Right this is what is going to happen. The two gang members, along with the mad old man, will be driven down to the port where they will board the overnight ferry to Dublin. The Irish police and customs know that they are on their way. All documentation to follow. As far as they know, the three of them are important witnesses in a highly sensitive court hearing. Accommodation and funds have all been agreed and finalised. These three will be accompanied all the way to Dublin and beyond, where a handler will take over responsibility. Once again hopefully that is the last we shall see or hear from them again.'

Chapter Sixteen

L ilian spoke quickly. 'Carperhanus?, it's getting late I need to go back to my house. But what happened to those on the container ship? And did they find any gunpowder?'

Carperhanus smiled and said, 'you will have to wait for the next bit. Good night Lillian.'

It was early, the sun was up and moving slowly across the sky with not a cloud in sight. Still bouncing like a rubber ball, Lilian flew into the garden and as she got close to Carperhanus, his smile was a welcoming sight. Seated exactly as they were yesterday, were her closest friends. If you did not know any different, you would think that they had been there all night. They heard, 'morning all' from a cheerful Lilian. 'We are all ready, Carperhanus and we are so excited.'

'All right, here's what happened...'

Down in the cells.

Stickit hollered, 'out now! One at a time. Bok Choy and Charlie Parsnip, stay where you are.'

There were groans, mumbles and sulks, but no time to express themselves as Nickam pushed, shoved and manhandled them up the stairs, through a side door and into waiting unmarked police vans. The minute all six were bundled into a dark enclosed space, uproar and chaos broke out. Shouting everything from, 'where are you taking us? What about our clothes and stuff? We want our money from the bank. This is against the law. You lot are breaking the law.'

Nickam was smiling and laughing at the same time.

'You lot are going on a nice long cruise. You won't need money when you get there.' Still smiling he continued, 'I never thought I would see the day when I would say bye-bye.'

As the vans' doors were slammed shut and bolted, they continued to bang on the side of the vans.

Once it was out of the compound, their noise diminished as the lights of the van disappeared. Nickam, Stickit and two female PCs all breathed a sigh of relief.

'If we ever see them again', they agreed, 'we are quitting the force.'

It was quiet, too quiet, as the three slumped in the interview room. There were no windows, only a door that was bolted. Bok Choy had his eyes half closed, pretending to look at the floor. Charlie Parsnip seemed to be in a trance, sort of looking up at the ceiling. Now Old Joe sat on a hard bench, with a big smile on his face. He had been like that for over half an hour. Suddenly he jumped up shouting, 'I have a plan.'

The other two looked at him, both thinking, daft old fool. His speech was clear, and precise with a hint of eccentric.

'Look I have been weighing up our situation. Not too far from this station, I have an aunt. Who has a fairly big ramshackle old coach house. She would hide and look after us, I know she would. All we have to do is get out of here. Now if I lay on the floor, you two shout for help. Tell them I have conked out and need a doctor urgently. There could be a fairly good chance that they may leave the door open. If they don't I will stuff this bit of cardboard in the lock. Before I came in here, I had noticed that underneath the stairs that lead out of here, are paint brushes, dust sheets etc. and wait for it, workman's overalls. We dress up as painters and decorators, grab a tin of paint and some brushes and calmly walk up the stairs and out of the back door.'

The police station was back to its normal self. Quiet and peaceful, now that the nine in the basement had departed. But, and there is always a but, it was twenty minutes later that one of the young female PCs knocked softly on Commander Carl Shoebag's door to explain that the three that were due to go to Dublin had dressed in workman's clothes, disguised as painters and decorators, had walked out and vanished.

Carperhanus looked at Lilian and her friends and then went on to explain, with a big grin on his face, that the police station was never the same again.

Chapter Seventeen

On the run.

The sheets on the bed were as white as snow, crisp and soft to touch. Old Joe eased himself down on the sheets. They were cold to his touch but sheer luxury. They had made it to his aunt's house with more luck than judgement. Cold tired hungry, thirsty and in desperate need of help. His Aunt Flora known to all as Floradix, came from his mother's side of the family. After several bangs on the door knocker she opened up and had welcomed them in with open arms. Flora hugged them all, but knew better than to ask any questions.

As it was late they enjoyed a hot drink and biscuits and then all three were shown to their bedrooms. One house rule was a must. Smoking if you have to, outside only. Old Joe loved the feel of the sheets which bought back memories of his past. How long had it been since I had clean sheets to sleep in. He wondered if the other two had clean sheets.

'Now what was their names? Something Parsnip and the other one, Bok. Oh I can't remember. Who in their right mind calls their kids Parsnip and Bok? It sounds like a Chinese soup to me. Still talking to himself. Well I suppose I should get ready for bed. Shoes off first, can't get into bed and put my dirty shoes on these clean sheets, now can I. But I am not taking my socks off. One always seems to disappear. You go to your sock draw and what have you got? One sock. That is fine if you only have one foot. Once I went fishing, when I was young, yes okay I fell in. My socks got wet but they soon dried on my feet, so you could say they have had good wash. I took my shirt off once, before getting into bed and it was gone in the morning. I won't be doing that again. Now where are my tablets? I think there is one for my left leg, to stop it shaking itself about and another tablet to remove excess whistling from my ear. I keep thinking of the sheets, my aunt er… what's her name? put on the bed. Those sheets in the home looked grey, maybe to match the walls. Aunt Flora, got it, and the smell of stale tobacco mixed with the smell of rotten cabbage and the pillow, blankets all smelt the same.

I am sure that dollop, Tinsnap altered my tablets once. She gave me two green ones before I went to bed. I went to sleep okay but woke in the night thinking I was a chicken. That did put the wind up me, I can tell you. If I ever see green tablets I drop them in the gaps between the floor boards. Let the mice chew them I say. If the mice turn into chickens they won't get through the gaps in the floor.

Now, where is the light switch? Or should I leave it on? In the home you could not leave the light on. That dollop, Tinsnap removed all the bulbs. I wonder what she did with all the money? Probably spent it on Woodbines knowing her…

Well, it's been a long day. I wonder where the others are and if they have clean sheets. I bet the Pope is shouting and moaning as usual. I do miss my pipe and tobacco. I will leave the light on. I say good night to all my friends but I am not saying anything to that dollop, Tinsnap.'

The End.

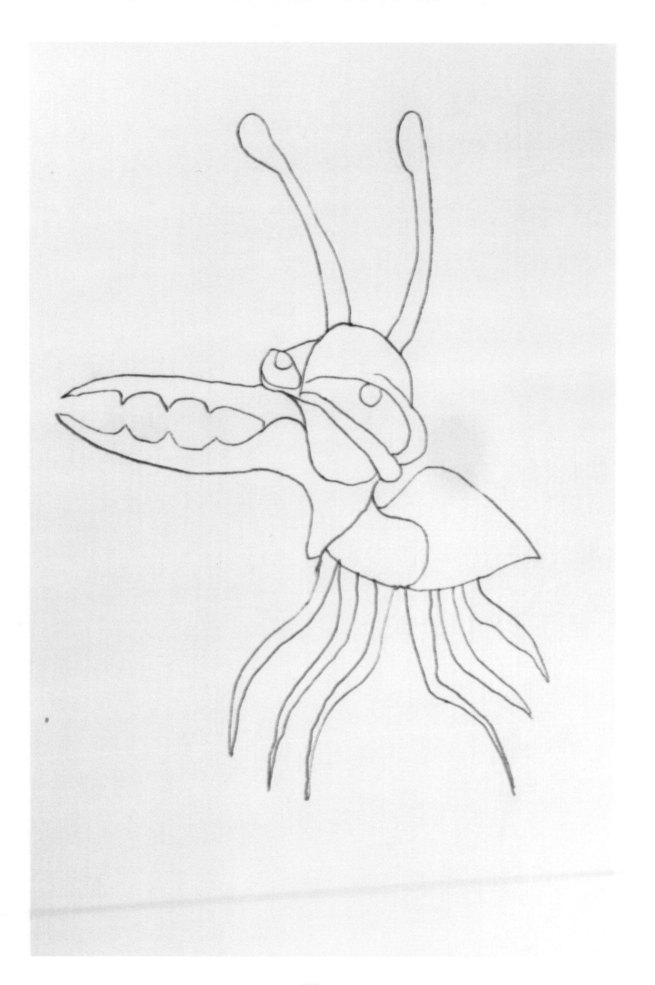

Printed in Great Britain
by Amazon

26546071R00041